Spirits of the Times

ISBN: 1-4515-0263-X
ISBN-13: 9781451502633

Spirits of the Times

Edmund Narine

2010

Dedication

For Lloyd Best

CONTENTS

PREFACE

This collection of short stories was assembled over the past two decades with the insistence of my dear wife, Samali Nakato Kajubi. It was a period when at different times I was preoccupied with two political whims—the creation of a federal system of government for Uganda and the reconfiguration of the political, economic, and administrative structures of Trinidad and Tobago. In essence, *Zeitgeist*, written in 2009, encapsulates the conditions driving my political ambitions in Trinidad and Tobago.

Makandal Daaga, written in 1989 depicts the Gothic in the African experience while exploring one man's trauma in a quest to rekindle the search for his African roots. The rewritten version is rooted in my conviction in the value of the story.

A Douen for Marie, Lovina's Grandson, and How Papa Bois Get Horn satisfies the imaginative exploration of the thorny and tricky situations which ensue when individuals are confronted with the reality of the folkloric spirits which inhabit the rain forests of Trinidad's Northern Range. Stories of these confrontations have entertained, fascinated, and terrified the faint-hearted amongst us, and pushed me to delve into that world of the mythical.

The publishing of this collection has pre-empted its eventual entry into the world of the warbenes, the denizens of Trinidad's once pristine rain forest streams. I suspect that at least one story will provide a moment of pleasure and satisfaction to the intrepid. Thus, I have dusted off the collection and, with an apology to the warbenes, present-ed this book to you.

Boston, Massachusetts
August 14, 2010

DESCRIPTION/NARRATIVE
SPIRITS OF THE TIMES

You do not see the chameleon but he sees you, perched on the branch of the samaan tree whose girth you pause to admire; and just as you fail to see the chameleon an arms-length above your head, so to you fail to see Papa Bois, the creature with the ram's head and the body of a man staring from his abode, inside the clump of bamboo growing on the banks of the dry ravine. He is hiding from you, for he knows, one glimpse of him would force you to shout "How Papa Bois get horn?" Read this book and you will be amazed at how 'Papa Bois get horn'.

This book, like the rainforest of Trinidad's Northern Range, takes the unwary visitor on a journey starting at the Dry River, paved and channeling through Port-of-Spain's urban ghetto from its source high up on the heights of El Tucuche, Trinidad's second highest peak. From El Tucuche one would see the distant horizon merge with the turquoise waters of the Paria Gulf. Cup a hand to the ear and be rewarded to hear drums throbbing in ceremonial obeisance to Shango, Lord of Thunder and of Lightning.

But one must not tarry, for it is here, too, high up on this magnificently foliaged mountain; here, where the immortelle flashes its flaming swords in March; and when the poui ring out its yellow bells in a high wind in April that one might suddenly encounter a douen—a spirit, a child wearing wide brimmed straw hat, its feet turned backwards as it awaits the night and the capture of an unwary child, and the pleasure that child brings when it falls from the high cliffs to the jagged rocks below.

Be adventurous. Take a trip any night on a Mayaro back road and come face-to-face with a lagahoo, a reader of books on the occult whose knowledge has empowered him to transform from elephant pig to buffalo dog at midnight.

'Spirits of the Times' is about rain forest spirits, urban ghetto politics, and rituals to Lord Shango. Not a book for the faint-hearted, but one can read it, and savor the consequences of fool hardiness.

Lovina's Grandson

I was ten years old when my Grandfather, Dougla, die and leave me without family in the village. Four years earlier my mother had run away from my father, and a year after she run-away, my father die when he try to cut a balisier for the PNM march on Chaguaramas and a mappippire bite him.

I stay with different villagers for a few months until they locate my grandmother and they put me on a train to go and live with her in Chaguanas.

When the train stop, I couldn't tell who was to pick me up, but it didn't take too long for me to find out, because the minute I hop off, two dark women head in my direction. One was short and stout, and she keep smiling even though she was missing three front teeth. The other woman frighten me. She looked like somebody who could eat bachac and ask for lagniappe. She was thin and tall, with long arms like a spider, a big calabash for a head, and broad feet bursting out from her alphagats.

The women reach me, and the big calabash-head lady shout, "Grandson! You look so big. Come boy, lemme kiss you." I feel like jumping back on the train, but I smile and let her dribble all over my face while Miss Three-teeth-missing clap she hands and laugh so hard I thought she win a whe-whe mark.

"I am Lovina, your grandmother," Miss Calabash-head say. "And this is Miss Agatha, she is…"

"You can call me Agatha, boy, I ain't one of them women who want handle to mih name, nuh."

Is funny how a simple remark like that could make you like somebody. I wish Agatha was my grandmother, but because Lovina was already that, I had to settle for she.

It seem we walk down the cane field road for hours before we reach a board house with a collapse roof in the centre of five or six mango trees. A coconut tree, bushy head and bend-over like my school master, look down on the mango trees as if he ready to beat them at the slightest move. And as if to keep the frighten mango trees from running away, a thick coreilly vine plaited into a chicken wire fence surround them on all sides. I turn from the board house and look around. The cane field road was a black hole, and acres and acres of sugarcane wave back at me. I never live near cane and I hated it.

Mr. Boucher was at the opening in the coreilly fence. Lovina and Agatha turn their face from him, but I say, "Morning, Mr. Boucher." When Lovina cuff me at the back of my head, Mr. Boucher raise his face to the sky and howl like a dog. I know his name was Mr. Boucher because Lovina and Agatha talk about him all the way from the train station. Lovina say he is a Lagahoo, and that sometimes he turn into a horse, other times a pig the size of an elephant, and at night he run up and down the cane field road. I smiled with Mr. Boucher because I fraid him. His face look like a crying black mask. I thought maybe one night when I coming home late and he turn into a pig-elephant he might recognize me and leave me alone.

We reach Lovina's house and I take one look at it and feel to run back up the cane field road and catch the train.

Lianas grip the mud walls, and the padlock on the front door was too big and shiny. My father stories about Jumbies and Souccouyant jump into my head. Three black pigs squealed in the pen with the low concrete wall that somebody start to build and never finish. Two goats bleated, and a black dog howled. What I notice fast about the animals is that, except for the black dog, they was thin and bony. The goats look like God-horse with horns. The front yard breadfruit tree was a skeleton, but the back yard mango tree was full with leaf.

I went to bed that night and wake about twenty-five times from animal noise and bad dreams about that place. In one dream, Mr. Boucher was a stallion squealing and pounding down the cane field road after me.

The next morning Lovina wake me up early and send me to feed the animals. About eight o'clock she wrap a piece of bake-and-salt fish, put it in my pocket, and send me off to a school that was about three miles away at the end of the cane field. When I come home in the evening, I feed the animals and, with Blackman, the dog, trying to catch me, I run up and down the cane field road until Lovina call me, give me a dry hops bread and a cup of bush tea, cuff me behind my head, and send me bawling to sleep.

This was my life day in and day out. I wonder why they had to send me to Lovina. What about my uncle they say I had in Point Cumana? I think a lot about running away and going to my uncle's house. Trouble is I only know his name as Boysie, and I don't have his address.

But I take my work seriously. I get up earlier than Lovina and feed the animals, but no matter how much I feed them, they wouldn't get fat. I cut water grass for them, pangola grass for them, and every day I take the goats for a graze along the cane field road. On weekends I take the pigs one by one on the road, but they own-way, they jump and scream and try to escape.

Anyway, things start to change when one day I come home from school and slip unnoticed under the house. I was wondering about how to get to my Uncle Boysie house in Point Cumana, when I hear Lovina and Agatha talking.

"But he seems to be a nice little fellow, Lovina. Why you want him to leave?" Agatha say.

"I want him to leave because is he who introduce Boucher to my pigs! Yesterday I see Boucher watching mih goats. And when I look at him, he laugh and howl 'The goats getting fat.' Now tell me what he mean?"

"But that ain't have nothing to do with that little boy. He does work hard feeding the animals."

"Agatha! You too stupid, you know. That is why you always get into trouble. You trust people too much. If you was like me, your husband woulda never clear out the house with the two old chairs and the fibre mattress and leave you to sleep on the floor."

"But Lovina, this is a little boy...."

"He is a little Coolie boy. And he just like he Coolie mother. You see how she run away and leave mih son and cause snake to bite him? Run away with a man. That's what!"

Well, I really make up my mind to find my uncle Uncle Boysie in Point Cumana. So I crawl out from under the house with Blackman and go up the road and hide in a cane patch to wait for Miss Agatha to pass.

Darkness was rolling in on the waving cane field when I spot Miss Agatha waddling up the road. I wait till she pass me and Blackman before I tip-toe behind her and shout "Miss Agatha!"

"Oh God! Ah Dead! Father! Heavens!" she shout before she look around and see me and Blackman.

"I need your help, Miss Agatha. I want to go to my uncle in Point Cumana."

"Listen boy! You coulda give me a heart attack. Like what Lovina say is true? You is a bad little Coolie boy."

"But Miss Agatha…. Miss Agatha, I sorry to frighten you, but I have to find mih uncle. And is only you I could ask. You know how to get to point Point Cumana. You…will know which house to ask for."

"Lord, Jesus! My heart still pounding," Miss Agatha moaned.

"I don't know his address, Miss Agatha, but I know his name. The first person I see I will say, 'You know a mister by the name of Boysie?'"

"And you think you will find him so?" Miss Agatha puff. "First thing you must understand is your uncle name is Boysie Handsome Butcher. Some people call him Boysie. Others call him Handsome—don't ask me why. And more people call him Butcher. So the person you ask for Boysie might know him as Handsome or Butcher. That is a hard way to find somebody. That is like looking for three people. And wait, he have another name, Heads. That man take after he mother, Lovina. In a big head contest is Lovina first and Heads second."

"But then what I must do now? Stay with Lovina? Maybe I should talk to Mr. Boucher and…."

"Look here. Boy! Keep away from that Lagahoo. You brave, you know? You know that man could turn you into a goat?"

"But is either I stay with Lovina or get help. I ask you, and you can't help, so maybe I should ask Mr. Boucher."

"Wait!" Agatha say. "I have a idea. You know Lovina pigs and goats thin like zwill? Well, let me ask you this, you know is Boucher who have them so?"

"Boucher have them so? But I does feed them. I cut water grass…"

"Boy, you don't understand," Agatha say, "Boucher sucking the blood from Lovina animals, and Lovina afraid to say something to him!"

"But…why she afraid? Agatha, how you know all this?"

"Because who else would suck Lovina animals dry. You tell me that! Who else will suck them goats dry? And you know what? Go and check all them animal neck. I sure you will find…"

"Oh, gosh! Miss Agatha…You frighten me. You mean Boucher is a Soucouyant, a bloodsucker, too?"

"And if I was you, instead of chasing down your Uncle Boysie like Blackman chasing down a mongoose in the cane field, I would stop talking to Boucher. Show him that you vex with him. Throw some threats. When you pass him by his gate, you could shout, "I will kill the Soucouyant that sucking Lovina goats and pigs when I catch him!" That will stop Boucher, and when he stop, you know what, Lovina bound to be grateful to you. You will make your grand-mother a friend!"

"But Miss Agatha, I is only ten. You think I can frighten…"

"Ai, boy, you notice something? The sun gone down. Do me a favour, doodoo, walk me to the junction."

"But, Miss Agatha, I fraid, too."

"Fraid for what? Look a penny. Come, Papa. Walk me to the junction."

"But who will walk me back?"

"You have Blackman. He's a big black dog. Lagahoo fraid of black dog. Here. Come, doodoo. Take the penny."

With that Miss Agatha grip my hand and I grip Black-man chain and in the darkness the three of we went fast up the cane field road.

On my way back down, I was so frighten that three times me and Blackman leave the road and dive in the cane field to hide from Mr. Boucher. The first time we dive Mr. Boucher was a donkey galloping and braying. The second time he was a horse, a real race horse galloping down the canefield road. And the third time he was a cow, ringing a bell and rattling a chain.

By the time I reach Lovina house I tell myself that I have to act like I ain't afraid of Boucher or else I will never make Lovina my friend. And if she wasn't my friend and I can't find my uncle, I would have to live with cuffs day and night. So it seem as if I have to threaten Boucher. But then suppose now it ain't Boucher who was the Soucouyant? Suppose Boucher was just a Lagahoo, and the Soucouyant was from Moruga, Erin, or Guayaguayare?

Again that night I wake up about twenty-five times to escape Boucher. In one dream he grip my shirt collar, pull me inside his yard, and try to bite my throat. I wake up in a sweat and make a few attempts to call Lovina in the next room, but I so fraid she cuff my head off that I stay quiet and try to stay awake instead..

But who could sleep in a place like that anyway? Whole night horses galloping, pigs squealing, goats bawling, Blackman howling, and in the morning, cuffs and more cuffs behind my head.

Well, I couldn't take it anymore, and so a few weeks later I decide to set a trap for Boucher the Soucouyant. First thing I do is get a Solo bottle, put a cloth wick in it, and full up the bottle with kerosene. Then I borrow a box of match when Lovina wasn't looking and hide it in my pocket.

The following night, around midnight, I get off my sugar and rice bags bed and, trembling, I make my way to the front door and the latch that Lovina throw every night. Lovina wasn't snoring, but I had to take my chance because sometimes she snore and sometimes she so quiet you could swear she ain't home.

"Where you going!" Lovina say from her open door in the darkness.

"Lovina, I going to pee."

"Twelve o'clock in the night you going outside to pee? This is the first time or you does do this every night?"

"Only tonight, Lovina."

"Well, don't go outside to pee. Whenever you want to pee, use the po. Here, keep it at your bedside."

I never feel so frighten in my life. I use the po and went back to bed and decide to make another plan. Another walk through the front door and Lovina would find me out. I lay in the darkness thinking that maybe I should sneak out the side window. But then a better plan enter my mind. Lovina floor boards was loose, so all I had to do was raise two boards up and let myself under the house. The good thing is Blackman always tie under the house, and I could get protection from him. So, I settle on that plan.

A few nights later, around midnight, I get up from my bed and quiet like bachac cutting a periwinkle flower, I move two boards from the floor. Then feeling around I find the bottle of kerosene and put the box of match in my pocket. Swinging my legs down I nearly give my self away when Blackman start to lick my foot and tickle me. I wanted to scream, but I bite my lip, drop to the ground, and went behind the water barrel at the side of the house to hide and wait for the Soucouyant to come.

I wasn't counting, but it seem like after ten mosquito bite, I hear a horse galloping down the canefield road. Boucher! I thought. I didn't expect this. I expect to see a ball of fire, a Soucouyant. Blackman growl, but he stop when I squeeze he mouth shut. The galloping get louder and closer. I grab the Solo bottle, pull a match from the box, and get ready to light the bottle wick and throw it at the beast when the pounding stop and a woman shout, "Lovina! Is Agatha. Lovina, wake up! Is Agatha!"

I get so damn confuse that I forget to tie Blackman to the pillar before I jump up and haul myself into my room. Fast like lightning, I replace the floor boards, spread the sugar bags, lie down, and act as if I fast asleep.

"Boy! You boy! Wake up! You don't hear somebody outside? You lazy boy, wake up before I cuff your head off! Get that dog before he bite Agatha. See what she want."

I scramble from my bed and run down the steps to the yard and catch Blackman and tie him up. Then I call out to Miss Agatha in the darkness.

"Miss Agatha, is me! What happen? What you want?"

"You tie the dog?"

"Yes. What you want?"

"Come closer, doodoo. Boy you look tall in your pajamas!" Miss Agatha shout, then she hold me and whisper in my ear "My child, mih husband come back and he tell mih to come and borrow a two dollars from Lovina. He want a little drink."

"But you come at this hour to get rum money? You riding a donkey?"

"Me ride a donkey? Boy, is a donkey cart I come in. Is me and mih compere. Go quick and tell Lovina to send a two dollars and lend me. And listen, doodoo, don't say mih husband come back, eh. Because you know Lovina, she don't like him, and if I have to dead, she would never lend me two dollars if she know I take him back."

So with that I went back in the house, give Lovina the story, and before long, Miss Agatha was on she way up the canefield road with the two dollars.

⚜

But I didn't wait long to get back into action. The next night I remove the floor boards, swing down to the ground, and take up mih post behind the water barrel with Blackman.

But I was too early, and so I take my mosquito bites and listen to crapaud singing from the roadside drain. Then around midnight a jumbie bird hoot and shut up the crapaud singers. I could hardly see in the half-moon light, but I strain my eyes and make out the mango tree hanging down like it praying above the pig pen and the unfinished concrete wall, and with Blackman at my side, I sit quiet like the crapaud and listen. Nothing happen and the crapaud start to sing again. I listen to them, and musta doze off when a screech from the jumbie bird lance the air. I jump up and hit my head against the floor boards. It seemed like something catch the bird, and it was beating its wings and struggling to escape. In two-twos the struggle was over and we, Blackman, the crapaud, the pigs, and the goats just listen and wait for I didn't know what.

Then suddenly the flapping of big wings full up the air. Blackman start to bark and the whole world explode with pigs squealing and goats bawling. A second later the sound of the wings fade, only to pick up and fade again. I realize then that the thing was flying around the house. When it land on the galvanise roof of the pig pen, the pigs went crazy and I grab my Solo bottle, the match-box and a match and get ready to strike it. Please, God, I prayed, let me catch Boucher and make Lovina happy for once. So I strike the match, light the wick, and pelt the Solo bottle at the low concrete wall.

"Vroom!" the bottle explode and turn the whole place into daylight. Blackman bolt for the Soucouyant on the pig pen roof, and I rush forward to make certain that that Soucouyant was Mr. Boucher. But I pee my pants when I see the thing lift from the pig pen roof and streak off in the sky. It was human, looking red and bloody like raw meat, with long, thin arms, broad feet, huge wings, and a big calabash-head glowing like a fire ball.

"Oh God! Is Lovina!" I screamed.

With the pigs squealing, the goats bawling, and Blackman barking, I run under the house and pull myself up through the opening in the floor and get inside the house. I left my room and rush to Lovina door. It was latched on the inside so I kick it down, because I know Lovina wasn't there. The room smell like a skinned snake, and I vomited. But I was determined to finish the job I start. I pull myself together, lit a match, and held it above my head. Lovina was no where in sight, but coils and coils of red skin was heaped on her mattress. The match went out. I strike another one and light the lamp. Then I went to the front door and throw it open. In a flash Blackman was inside. I grab his chain, put the lamp on a chair, and edge closer to look at the coils of skin when something crash on the house. I screamed, and in my dash to escape I accidentally knock Lovina kerosene lamp to the floor. I reach for the lamp but it was too late—fire was spreading across the board floor. Lovina was on the roof, and I knew I had to get away. I ran from the room and tumble down the steps in the darkness. Somebody laugh, and then a dog howl. It was Mr. Boucher. I see him in the glow from the burning house, dress in a white gown and, holding a bamboo rod like a wire walker for balance, he staggered across the coreilly fence.

I was horrfied. "Oii!" I cried, and with Blackman at my side speed up the canefield road.

When Blackman and I come to a stop about a quarter mile away, I look back towards Lovina house. Daggers of fire was stabbing up the air and making the cane leaves look like ripe figs. I sit down and rest and watch the burning house set fire to the breadfruit tree before I pick myself up, and, with Blackman chain in my hand, I run from the cane field knowing that no matter how much time it take, and whether my uncle name was Heads, Handsome, Boysie, or Butcher, me and Blackman was heading for one place— Point Cumana.

How Papa Bois Get Horn

Ever since the beginning of Trinidad time, people have wondered where Papa Bois came from and why he was created with a goat's head and a man's body.

Some people say he was born in Blanchisseuse, others say he was born in Maracas. Some say he was a Spaniard who deserted Columbus when he landed at Erin to stock up on fresh water in 1498. Still others say he came to Trinidad with the first French settlers in 1777, and they point to his name, Bois, as proof of their claim.

Nowadays, folklorists say that Papa Bois was a Carib Indian who was born and raised in Arima. Proof of that they say was found in the Middens, the Caribs' rubbish dumps.

While I do not know where Papa Bois was born, my grandfather, Besson they call him, tell me what happened to turn Papa Bois into a ram man.

Papa Bois, Besson say, was a nice man, a sweet bread. Good looking and hard working, he planted acres of cassava and pigeon peas on the hillsides of the Northern Range; and when the cassava crop was fat, he would grate the cassava and make pone and cassava bread for his neighbor Boysie and Boysie wife. And then at Carnival time when the pigeon peas was fat like chennit seeds, he would pick and shell peas, kill a fowl, and make chicken pelau for Boysie and his wife to take to Port-of-Spain to see mas'.

Besson say he thought all that was good, and he told Papa Bois so. But when one day Boysie cry out for belly pain and Papa Bois send his wife Rosa to rub Boysie belly, Besson shook his head in protest.

"Papa Bois," Besson say, "you is the only man in the whole world who will send his wife to rub his friend belly. And Rosa is the prettiest woman in Trinidad! If Trinidad ever get a princess, Rosa would be she. And you letting her rub Boysie belly? You going too far. Check up on yourself, Papa Bois. You looking for trouble."

"But Boysie is mih friend," Papa Bois say.

"Friend or no friend," Besson say, "It ain't have friend where wife concern."

And so each time Papa Bois send his wife to rub Boysie belly, Besson complain. Then one day, when pommecythere was falling like golden eggs and Papa Bois wife went to Rio Claro to visit she macomey, a belly pain take Papa Bois, and even though he drink two cups of lime-bud tea with cinnamon and nutmeg, his belly pain seemed to get stronger. When the pain became so strong that even Papa Bois could not take it any longer, he cried out to his neighbors.

"Ai, Boysie, send your wife to rub mih belly for me. I eat too much green guava and mih belly killing me."

"She coming!" Boysie shout, but he kept the door to his carat house locked tight. Each time Papa Bois cry out to Boysie for help, Boysie would shout "She coming!"

Boysie never send his wife to help Papa Bois. And when at daybreak Papa Bois's wife, Rosa, returned from Rio Claro, she hot up some soft candle and coconut oil and give Papa Bois a good belly rubdown. Yet rub as hard and as often as she could, Papa Bois's bellyache remained as strong as the day it started.

Besson say he was real sorry for Papa Bois. He believed somebody was doing him bad and he tell him so.

"Papa Bois, that ain't sound like no normal belly pain you have there, you know?" Besson say. "A normal belly don't growl like your own. Whenever I touch your belly, I hear a dog growl as if it want to bite me. That dog have to come out, Papa Bois. Somebody do you bad and put a dog in your belly. And that dog have to go. I don't care what you say, Papa Bois, in the morning you and me heading for Mayaro to see 'bout you!"

And so, the following day, with a heavy heart and a big bellyache, Papa Bois and Besson set out for Mayaro with a vial of lavender, a pint of castor oil, a bottle of white rum, and a package of asofoetida, the things some people carry to Mayaro for a jumbie cure.

Two days later, Papa Bois was cured. He was so happy that on the way home he stop and buy a pair of white crepsoles for Rosa. And when Besson ask why he didn't buy flowers instead, Papa Bois say that Rosa always in one shoe because she must of lost the other one. Well, that wasn't a good enough explanation for Besson, but he say he and Papa Bois return home happier than a grap of sickia in a ripening rose mango tree.

Besson say with the box of crepsoles under his arm, Papa Bois run up the steps, pull the door open and shout, "Rosa! Rosa! I home, girl. Papa Bois cured!"

Besson say he run up the steps too but the door slam shut just as Papa Bois scream out, "Oh God, Rosa! What you doing to Boysie?" And Besson hear Rosa say with a girlish giggle, "I rubbing he belly. That is all, and he like it."

Besson say he scrambled to the back yard just in time to see Boysie drop from a window and disappear like a zandolee in Papa Bois's cassava garden.

For days Papa Bois disappear from the village. And whenever Besson would go looking for him and knock on his door, Rosa would come out and say, "I ain't know where he gone, nuh."

And when Besson would ask if Papa Bois had gone back to Mayaro, Rosa would shrug her shoulders, smile, and say, "Me ain't know."

Then days turned into weeks and weeks into months. All Souls Day came and went. Christmas come and gone. And still, no Papa Bois in sight. And then Carnival day arrived in an early morning Jour Vert, when the sun was barely peeping over the roocoo trees, and Robbers and Kalinda men were on the road ramajaying and bussing head, Besson set out for Papa Bois's house to take a last try at getting to the bottom of his disappearance.

When he reach the rum shop, Besson say he spot Rosa, dress like a La Diablesse in her Jour Vert costume—a white bonnet and white dress with the hem sweeping onto the ground. "Oh God, boy! Rosa pretty!" Besson say he whisper to himself. "I wish Papa Bois wasn't mih friend."

He say Rosa make him feel to make a move to capture she right there on the village road.

Besson say it was about then when his attention turn from Rosa he see the Jour Vert mas' player standing behind her. The fella was dressed in a new pair of crepsoles, ragged dirty khaki pants, a black goat-skin coat, and a black felt hat on his head.

"Good mas'," Besson say and turn to Rosa. "Rosa, who is the mas' man next to you. He looking real good, you know. He have a first prize to win. By the way, Papa Bois come home yet?

Besson say Rosa smile, look up and down the road, and then say to him, "Come and see who it is, nuh."

Besson say he step forward, and as he get closer he had to wrinkle his nose from the strong ram-goat stench coming from the mas' man. Besson say he put out he hand to greet the Jour Vert player, but instead of the mas' man saying something like, "Good morning, God Brother," the mas' man just keep chewing gum and watching him.

So Besson pull back he hand and say, "What happening there, partner? You looking good, real good. But—Ai! You look like Papa…." Besson say the words stick in his throat and he take a fast look at Rosa for explanation. But Rosa watch him and the fella and giggle.

"This fella, Rosa…. Ai…he whole face have hair. What happen, he don't shave? Who is he?" Besson demanded.

"Take off he hat, nuh," Rosa laugh, "you might make him out." Besson say he wanted to run, but quick, quick, he move forward and knock the felt hat from the fella head.

"Oh God, no!" Besson say he bawl when he recognize Papa Bois with his hairy face, ram-goat beard, and a pair of dagger-like horns.

Besson say Papa Bois recognize him too and tried to talk, but all he could say was, "Behh. Behh. Behh." Besson say he was frightened for so, but the last thing Rosa feel was fear. She grab Papa Bois hand, raise her skirt and run shrieking down the village road.

Besson say he stand in front the rum shop shaking like a loose galvanize in a strong wind. For the first time he had seen Rosa legs, and it was then that he understand why she always wear a long dress with a crepsole on one foot. One leg was smooth, brown-skin and unblemished; while the other leg was black-and-white and hairy, with the hoof of a goat.

Makandal Daaga

Sonny Frederick, my father, was a quiet man who had been appointed heir to our religious tradition, one that required the courage to summon our mighty Lord, Shango, pay homage, then, in the presence of his awesome power, force his retreat to the sky. I was a participant to the events narrated here, events that would end in my father's demise. As I sit in this temple amidst the drummers and dancers, a celebration I organized to fulfill our Lord's wish—the adoption of my father and daughter's ancestral names—my thoughts return to the events I observed.

My father was witness to Shango's anger when, during a night of carousing, his brother in an attempt to usurp my father's position of High Priest had entered the sacred temple and summoned our Lord. My uncle went missing for five days before he was found, his neck wedged in the fork of a calabash tree, an hour's uphill walk in the forest above the temple, his flesh devoured by corbeaux. Nothing remained of my uncle except his skeleton—white bones gleaming in the hot sun. Even then my father, whether from fear or ignorance or intimidation, would not accept the responsibility of High Priest.

Yet Sonny had no choice, for it was he who had received the prophetic dream from Oloroon, God of Gods.

"Take the new name I shall give to you; then find the sacred thunderstone," Oloroon had commanded. "Go to the temple. Place the thunderstone on the altar, kneel before it, and summon your Lord. When the sky divides in the arch of his brilliance and the earth trembles upon his arrival, say, 'I am Babatunde, servant of Lord Shango!' Be quick. Draw your cutlass and slay the sacrificial goat. Fill the calabash and offer its blood; once fortified your Lord will test you—he shall refuse to return to the sky. And he will advance as if to destroy you. Be courageous. You have the amulet. You have the incense. Rattle your father's bones, splash incense in his eyes, and chant the words that will force his retreat to the sky."

⇥⇤

Thirty years as sexton at St. Christopher's Church did not erase my father's responsibility to act. He did not, he would not, even though Oloroon gave examples of the price for disobedience. In another dream Oloroon had instructed Sonny to name his first-born son Oshosi. My father departed from those instructions. He named his son Emanuel. When the child was four, Shopona, God of smallpox, destroyed Emanuel.

Reverend McLeod, pastor of St Christopher's at that time, named and christened all my father's children. I was the first child, and then came Emanuel, James, and John; They were not named Oshosi, Agangu, and Eshu – the hunter, volcano, and God of travelers – as Oloroon had instructed. My father had been commanded to name me Olossa, goddess of the lagoon. Reverend McLeod named me Clarissa, the name of his deceased mother. My father had sworn to obey Oloroon's commands. I knew that one day he would pay a terrible price for his disobedience.

⌖

My father was seven years old when his mother and father were implicated in the death of a priest. His mother was sentenced to life imprisonment, his father to death by hanging. During his trial my grandfather remained silent except at the end, before he was sentenced, when he was asked why he had committed such an abominable act, he simply said, "He interfered." My father was sent to his grandmother, a devout woman, who raised him to obey and witness for the Christian God.

Fifty years ago my father received Oloroon's command, and for those fifty years my father had shirked his responsibility while he hid behind the cross of St. Christopher. Even now as I sit in this temple, churning with dust and drumbeats and dancers, I search for the reasons for my father's inaction. Why did he desert our Gods, those who had cared and protected us from the first day we appeared on earth, on African soil?

⌖

I was two months pregnant when Lord Shango again showed his anger towards Sonny, for his refusal to change his name and reconnect to his ancestors. A small sore appeared above my left ankle. I thought nothing of it. The sore would soon disappear as it appeared, I thought. However, within days a small pus-filled cavity developed. I drew my father's attention to it.

"How long this going on?" he gasped.

"One week, Sonny," I said, shocked by his irrational response.

I thought I saw deep concern on his face, but quickly realized that it was fear, and like an infection, I too became afraid of what that sore could mean. Sonny washed the wound with care and then bandaged it with cloth soaked in iodine. Three days later he removed the bandage.

Pus oozed from a hole and dribbled onto my foot. Sonny looked into my eyes. We both knew what that meant—I would lose my leg, another price for Sonny's disobedience.

That day, as I lay on my bed, my father at my side, I could see the mid-day sun light up the trunk of a mango tree a stone's throw away. Desperate with fear, the massive mango trunk reminded me of the power of the leg I would now lose. I would never run up and down hills and jump village drains again. I reached out for the only hope that I had, that I believed in—Lord Shango. I looked at my father and saw the tenderness in his eyes.

"Oh God, Sonny, help me. Convert and change your name. Everything will be all right. Don't be always frightened. It is Oloroon's command that you take the position of High Priest, perform the rites, and adopt your ancestral name, Babatunde. Lord Shango will help us. Do as he commanded," I pleaded.

"You think so, Clarissa. And what about my job, my work at the church? Reverend McLeod will fire me; he will kick me out."

"Sonny, you remember what happened to your brother Boboy. Remember what happen to Emanuel. Why you so stubborn? Oloroon chose you; you must accept or he will destroy us one by one. He will destroy you; and he will destroy me!"

"I will christen your child, Clarissa. I go now to do Oloroon's bidding." Sonny bestirred himself. He picked up his jacket and Bible and departed my room. But whatever his intention, he must have remembered something important, for he suddenly reversed himself and reentered my room to place his Bible on the sofa before he headed out the door again.

"Sonny, what is it! Where are you going?" I shouted.

He ignored me and went out to the yard, rhythmically slapping his hands and chanting. I limped to the window and threw it open. Sonny stood in the middle of the yard, his eyes surveying the road, neighbor Job's house, Miss Thelma's house, and back to the yard in which he stood. A family of crows fluttered from the robust mango tree and settled on my clothesline. Sonny looked confident. I wanted to shout, "Sonny what are you doing?" but I bit my lip and held my speech. Sonny spread his jacket on the earth, kneeled on the jacket, and lifted his arms to the sky.

"Lord Shango," he cried, "Great God Shango. Take this pain from my child. Remove this iniquity from my daughter. My Lord, I beg of you. Oh, Shango, merciful God of Thunder and of Lightning, I have shirked my responsibilities. I have ducked my obligations. But I know it is never too late—today I accept my responsibility, my Lord. I am a new man, my Lord. And I shall do your bidding, my Lord. I will change my name and take responsibility for my people. Oh, my Lord Shango help me, help us. Please, oh Lord, help my daughter!"

Darkness descended in the fury of a tempest. The crows, terrified, as if the target of a shotgun blast, leapt to the sky. I watched my father, fascinated by the sudden change of weather. Sonny was in the middle of the yard, terrified, his arms outstretched as if nailed to a cross, the wind-whipped water drenching his body. Lightning flashed and thunder exploded as if in my room.

I heard Miss Thelma shout, "Clarissa, shut the window and stay inside!" I ignored her and looked towards the sky. Lightning, the shape of a scythe, flashed in a rumble of thunder. Fear gripped me for the storm seemed supernatural.

I shouted, "Sonny, quick. Run from the yard!" But I was too late. In the next instant a sword of lightning struck the mango tree—it exploded in a million chunks. Slivers of wood sailed through the air to crash on my house and the metal roofs of houses for miles around. The mango tree, once a gigantic umbrella, the home of birds and lizards and snakes, was reduced to a smoking hulk surrounded by a jumble of heavy logs.

Sonny went momentarily mad. And like a mad man he ran at full speed to escape his Lord. Heedless, he bumped onto mango log after mango log. He fell, picked himself up, started off and crashed onto the logs again. In his desperate effort to escape, Sonny, exhausted and momentarily mad, began to crawl like a caterpillar over the pileup of mismatched logs.

I stood at the window terrified; but fearing for my father's safety I shouted, "Sonny! Sonny! Over here!" And it was then that I realized that Sonny could not see, I was sure of it—my father had gone blind.

I ran from the house to my father's rescue. Devastation was everywhere. Large chunks of wood, hacked off by Lord Shango's shimmering sword, blocked my path and forced me to climb like a cat to reach him. He was whimpering and still crawling like a caterpillar. That he was alive was a miracle. I pulled him to his feet, and dragged him across the mango logs and onto the road. We must have looked like the walking dead as I limped and struggled to carry my blinded father towards the rectory. A half hour later we entered Sonny's room at St Christopher's. I dropped Sonny on his bed and switched on the radio. A reporter was on the air.

"Moments ago a flash thunderstorm demolished a number of houses in the Northwest sector of Trinidad. The debris from a tree struck by lightning covered a wide area. It is not unusual for flash thunderstorms to occur at this time of the year." The commotion had devastated me. I lost my child.

⚔

Three months passed. Sonny regained his sight and my leg healed. Sonny, however, had not fulfilled his pledge. From the scorched earth, where the mango tree stood, he had secured the sacred thunderstone, but he had not performed the sacred rites and changed his name as promised.

And as the wet season gave way to the dry, the two minds which were so long a part of Sonny's nature continued. My father could not comprehend the enormous damage his inaction was inflicting on our people. The absence of a High Priest had caused the faithful to stray. Once zealous worshippers of Lord Shango, they were now scattered like chips from the exploded mango tree. Some were Anglicans, Catholics, Muslims, while others were atheists. The people of Caroni were faithful to *Brahma* and *Shiva*, yet we had abandoned Lord Shango. I knew that some day Sonny would pay a bitter price for his indecision. I had become pregnant again but held it from my parents. And as I sit in this temple and watch the ceremony unfold before me, I remember how much I worried about what punishment Lord Shango would take against my child because of Sonny's failure to keep his promise.

Sonny was fifty-eight years old when I told him I was again pregnant.

"Oh, Clarissa!" he cried, "I have a name for she!" I was surprised. I thought that his concern would have been with punishment. I was eighteen and unmarried.

"But, Sonny," I said, "What is wrong with you? We don't know if it is a girl or a boy, and you are naming the child?"

"That is a girl, Clarissa, I know it. Oh, Lord Shango, we have a beautiful black baby girl—and her name…Clarissa, her name is Olossa!"

Beneath the rumble of the drums my thoughts tumble end over end as I recall these events. I watch the dancers leap in the air, their razor-sharp cutlasses slashing at unseen enemies. One accident and their white robes would be stained red. And in this moment, anger overwhelmed me as I thought about my father's feeble attempts to carry out his obligations.

Reverend Hailsmith was visiting as usual when, in conversation, he mentioned that St. Christopher's might be given a new name.

"But why the name change, Reverend? St. Christopher is a very good name to me," Sonny said.

"And that is exactly the problem," Reverend Hailsmith replied. "St. Christopher sounds right for the wrong people and wrong for the right people. Lord and Lady Robert Hastings have perceived a need for a larger church. They are quite willing to donate whatever monies are required for expansion. However, there is one caveat: they insist on a name change from St. Christopher to St. Margaret."

"You mean, Reverend, that's the only reason for changing the church name, people with money want the name changed?"

"Why! Of course, they want a name change in return for their donation. Can't find a better reason to change a name, can you?"

Sweat appeared on my father's face, and his khaki shirt was stained at the armpits. He swallowed his fear and continued.

"Reverend Hailsmith," Sonny said boldly, "I changing my name too."

"Nonsense! Son-Son. You have a perfectly good name. Sonny Frederick. Do you know who Frederick was? Ever heard of Frederick the Great? That's you! You are Frederick the Great!"

My father winced. "But Reverend Hailsmith, I have to change my name. I must!" he said desperately.

Sonny retreated as Reverend Hailsmith's steel blue eyes seemed to pierce his soul and deflate his courage.

"You must, eh. Do I hear mumbo jumbo? Do I hear talking drums? Look, Frederick, what the devil are you talking about?"

"Please, Reverend, I want you to christen me. I want you to change my name!"

The Reverend Hailsmith fell into a fit of laughter. "Christen you," he bellowed. "Give you a new name?"

"Yes, Reverend…. No, Reverend. I have a name. I mean yes. I want you to christen me. Christen me now! Right here! Right now. I have my name…."

"And what may I ask is your new name, my dear Sonny Frederick?" Reverend Hailsmith demeanor changed fast, like a twenty-four-hours going from green to brown. "Come, my dear Sonny Frederick, what is this new name that you speak of? Tell me, is it Matthew? Is it Mark? Is it Luke? Please, my dear man, pray tell me your new name."

My father's name exploded like a cannon ball from his mouth: "Daaga!"

"Daaga, Sonny Frederick, is your new name?"

"Yes. My new name is Daaga—Makandal Daaga!"

I was in the adjacent room and even now, at this frenzied moment, I could hear the peal of Reverend Hailsmith's laughter roll from my father's house with the departing reverend. I knew that the reverend was occasionally drunk, but this…Then I realized why some priests were killed. Even the earth-shaking beat of the drums could not drown out the sound of that bitter defeat.

But what was even more disturbing to me was Sonny's use of the name Daaga. Lord Oloroon had commanded he take the name Babatunde; Sonny preferred the name Daaga—Makandal Daaga, the name of the man who in 1837 led the unsuccessful mutiny of the First West India Regiment in Trinidad. Sonny was convinced that Daaga was the name for him. When I objected and reminded him of Lord Oloroon's command, he simply said, "Is an African name I take; Lord Oloroon will understand." That answer flabbergasted me. I could not believe how naïve my father was.

My mother then entered the room. I was never fond of her, and now, as she turned on my father, my feelings turned to hate. "Sonny, you crazy? You stone crazy? I hear you talking this madness, this stupidness, this shit about changing your name, I didn't know you serious. Since we married you preaching name change. Listen! I tell you already, I ain't no African. I born here in Trinidad, and I will dead here in Trinidad. You try your best to change the children name, and you fail. They not African either. And you see Clarissa, whenever she have a child, no African name for she, because she ain't no African!"

I listened to my mother, and I wondered what womb, what experience, what dreams, could create a woman like her—she and the friends who supported her. They sat and stared at my father like mourners before the open coffin at a wake.

One of the women, Miss Victoria, addressed my father. "Mr. Frederick, how come it is that out of this whole village of Bad Body Hill, is only you want to change your name? You say you is African. You say you had a dream. But African is black people!"

My father retorted, "So what you mean, I not black then? Well, let me give you some news. I! Me! You! We are all black. And we are all Africans, no matter what you say.

No matter what you think. No matter what you believe. We are all Africans!"

My father was like that. He vented his rage on everyone, except Sarah my mother. She was a lioness, with the rich brown color of that animal. She was the mixture of a French mother and African father, and she was ferocious. This was the woman who only six months earlier had played 'Mas' in George Bailey band, *Somewhere in New Guinea*. I often wondered what charm or guile my father used to capture her. We all knew that he was afraid of her.

"Miss Victoria, what you mean I ain't black?" Sonny said.

"That's what I mean. You not black. A little dark skin, yes. But not black. Is your wife black?"

"Miss Victoria, if I ain't black, then what color is me? White!"

"Sonny, look! What I mean is you ain't black, black, black! OK?"

My father groaned and surrendered the argument. I was at his side. The women watched him in silence. His eyes strayed on Mrs. Morgan, as if begging for her support. Mrs. Morgan roused herself, her beautiful face, enhanced by two coatings of flambeau soot, had an incredulous look on it.

"Oh, God," she said, looking vacantly at the floor, "imagine somebody have a good name like that, Sonny Frederick, and they want to change it—for what? Daaga!"

At the base of the mountain, in scattered, forest-hidden houses, I knew that our people, because of their ignorance of the history of our Lords, had become suspicious of temple activities. Many abhorred the blood sacrifices while imbibing the representation of that sacrifice on Sundays. Tonight, secured behind doors and windows scrawled with crosses, some will string cashew nuts and small sacks of indigo around the necks of their children while others will read Psalms and sing hymns to chase off the unknown evils.

The night sky seemed a body wrapped in purple shrouds. Like a pregnant woman, the full moon lowered itself onto the looming hills. I wondered how long, how many years would pass before the worship and veneration of our mighty Lords would again prevail among our people. I felt the heavy weight of hopelessness combined with the grief I suffered from the death of my father overwhelm me, and I wept.

I had tried my best to keep the news of my pregnancy from Sarah, but she found out, as I knew she eventually would. I believed that I would have to deal with her outrage. But I was wrong—I had to deal with her violence. Sarah slapped my face with the force of a zebra's kick.

My father was horrified as I crashed against the china cabinet. Broken tea cups, saucers, plates showered the floor. And to my surprise, my father grabbed Sarah and halted her attack on me.

"Sinful bitch!" Sarah screamed. "You…bringing a bastard to curse my house? You sinful bitch!"

She shook Sonny off, grabbed me by the hair and dragged me towards the open window.

Ten feet below, Reverend Hailsmith parked his Austin car, and, with a perpetual grin upon his face, started up the stairs. Sarah saw him through the open window. She dropped me, straightened her hair and frock, and went out to the landing to greet him.

"Good evening, Reverend," she cooed. "Good evening, sir."

"Oh, my dear sister Sarah, how gracious you look. The Lord has been very kind. Will you be visiting the rectory tonight for tomorrow's preparation? I'm sure Sonny will not take offense." He chuckled.

"Yes, Reverend. Praise the Lord. Sonny is taking a nap. I was just about to leave for the church."

"Well, please ride with me. What Sonny doesn't know he cannot object to, eh?" Reverend Hailsmith laughed.

* * *

The wump and thump of the drums tumbled towards a climax. Some spectators now pranced among the red bandeaux-headed worshippers while others continued to watch. I knew that our bodies, heated by the hot, humid tropical air and the soul-tearing rhythm of the drums, could only be cooled by the satiating blood of the sacrifice.

The saffron moon had climbed the hills and now embraced the liana-coiled temple. Exhausted worshippers were stacked like corpses upon the dusty temple floor. A young man leading a white goat entered the temple and sacrificed it.

I sat alone and I thought about the purpose behind this feast: the renaming of my daughter and her grandfather. They were both there, Olossa in the flesh; and Sonny, a spirit, reincarnated in a body lying on the floor.

In my thoughts I can see his face again. Oh, Sonny was so happy to hear my plan: a double christening.

"Oh, Clarissa. Clarissa, you are my daughter. You are my beloved daughter." He cried and hugged me. My father was so happy. So like a child. I knew that my plan was right, a double christening for two children.

That Sunday Sonny's rapture turned to rage when Sarah rejected my plan. Before dawn, under the cover of darkness, her footsteps sounded on the wood steps leading up to the veranda as she returned from the rectory. Sonny was waiting for her. He had suffered this indignity for years. I could hear him pacing his room. Today my father would stand or fall, I thought.

He greeted Sarah at the door. "Sarah," he said, "nine days from today I will change my name to Daaga, and I will change my granddaughter's name too, to Olossa. I am telling you now, because I tell everybody. The feast is ready. Today I end the indignity I have suffered these past years."

Oh, how a few words can turn a lifetime of death into a new beginning? I heard my father and my spirit soared. I eased out of bed, put on the dress at hand, and eyed them through the cracked bedroom door. I was surprised to see my father. He was shirtless and in his bare feet wearing his short white pants. A red bandeau was wrapped around his head.

"That is only part true," Sarah replied. "Your name will be Dag—whatever, but my granddaughter's name is Mary—Sarah Mary."

My father seemed to shrink in the dim light. He moaned. "Oh, God, Sarah, don't take this from me. Please, Sarah, don't take it from me."

I looked at Sarah. How beautiful she is, I thought. But I knew those sparkling eyes and voluptuous mouth were not only for my father to enjoy.

"Sonny!" she shouted, "my granddaughter's name is Mary Sarah Frederick! Reverend Hailsmith said so. I say so. God want it so! So who is you to say no?"

Sonny shook with rage. "I say so. I! Me! Daaga say so! African son. Warrior! I say so." Tears streamed down the gullies and ravines of his face.

"Sarah," he said calmly, "somebody will die today. Don't let it happen. Is four children we have. You name all four. This is my granddaughter. I say she name is Olossa, and it will be, if is over my dead body!"

"You know, Lord Hastings was right, Sonny. You is only man because you wear pants. So what is you?—And then you threatening me with death. Who are you?

"I am a man! Look at me. I am a man! But you," he whispered, "you are a whore. A righteous whore!" he screamed. "Go back to the reverend and sleep some more!"

Sarah slapped him hard. I stood petrified. A jumbie bird hooted, my baby whimpered—and then a sound like the rustling of unfolding feathers came to my ears. Death, I knew, was near.

Sonny leaped at Sarah, missed, and sprawled onto the kitchen floor. In a flash, he was on his feet like a tom cat. Blood oozed from his mouth. Sarah stalked him in silence, a lioness looking for an opening. Suddenly she lunged for his crotch, but he was swift. He broke her thrust, dashed towards the garden tools stored in a corner of the room, and before she could divine his intentions, a cutlass was grasped in his hand. Sarah recoiled. He raised the cutlass.

She threw her hands in the air and screamed, "Son-Son, no! No, Son-Son!"

"Daaga!" my father bellowed and swung the glinting blade. Sarah's head thumped to the floor. For a moment her body stood erect before it too collapsed onto the twitching head.

The deed done, my father leapt from the house and headed for the temple in which I now lie. I followed as fast as I could. He was no longer a tom cat, he was a lion. And suddenly I realized what that head-long rush to the temple meant. I cried out to him: "Sonny! Sonny! No! Your name!"

Minutes later we were on the upward-winding track high above the last houses on the mountain. In the early morning darkness I tripped and fell over logs and roots lying in my path. I was drenched in sweat, and near out of breath when I reached the temple.

Sonny was inside. Lighted flambeaux flickered along the aisle and around the circle used to drum and dance. He stood before the altar, at the far end of the circle. Horrified, I clung to a bamboo post and struggled with the urge to assist my father, but I knew my intervention would only be a delay in Sonny's eventual fate. From his pocket he withdrew the sacred thunderstone. He kissed it, placed it on the altar, then, his face lifted to the sky and his voice filled with emotion, he summoned our mighty Lord, Shango, God of Lightning and of Thunder.

In a brilliant flash the thunderstone exploded and knocked me to the ground. The temple's floor shook as though the earth was collapsing around us. Our Lord had arrived, and I, lying on the ground, raised my eyes to behold him and was momentarily blinded by his scintillating brilliance. And it was then, in a loud and eerie voice, like an echo crossing a great void, my father identified himself, "I am Daaga! Makandal Daaga, my Lord!"

"Oh God! Sonny, Sonny," I cried. "Not that name!" My father had made an unforgivable error. I knew it; and he realized it. "Forgive me, Lord," he cried. "Forgive me. My name is…Lord!" Sobbing, Sonny fell on his knees before the brilliant light. He had rites to perform; he had neglected them; and now he would pay.

The blinding light began to spin, and a roar erupted from the bosom of the earth. I heard my father cry, "Clarissa! My Lord forgive me! Clarissa!" The light burst into flame and set the temple on fire. Impulsively, I jumped to my feet and began to run. I missed the path and fell headlong into thick bush. I picked myself up, fell, and ran, and fell again.

Crazy with fear, I stopped to catch my breath and took a backward glance, and was surprised to neither see nor hear the fire I saw moments earlier razing the temple above. I stood rooted to the ground, my heart pounding, my body bruised, my red dress torn to shreds. Thoughts raced through my mind: Sonny's fate, Sarah's death, and above all, my own safety. I would have to find the path again and flee the wrath of our Lord. Sonny had brought this on himself; I knew he would be destroyed. And it was then, with those thoughts, in a flash, I realized the danger was not mine. I had nothing to fear.

I could tell daybreak was at hand. Under the thick bush and the intertwined branches of the bacanoit and mango, darkness prevailed. But overhead, through openings among the leaves, I could see grey clouds tinged with gold. I retraced my steps, picking my way through the undergrowth, and reached the temple just as virgin light painted the tops of the tallest trees.

I stopped at the entrance. The acrid smell of burnt hair and charred flesh filled the air. I searched along the aisle, around the circle where dancers and drummers once pounded the earth, under the bamboo seats, the latticed bamboo roof, but there was no sign of fire or my father's body. I wondered what part the altar, so silent, so like a tomb, would play in this search. And then something unusual caught my eyes—a small black mound. My heart skipped under my breath. I started towards it. And as I edged closer, I could see what I first thought to be a mound was in fact a pyramid, a small black pyramid. The sun burst upon the temple with the full glow of its cleansing light, and in that moment, that beginning day, I knelt and felt the charred remains, the pyramid of black ashes that was now my father. Embedded in the collapsed ash was a black, polished thunderstone.

The feast is over now. I have fulfilled Lord Oloroon's command—the adoption of ancestral names for my daughter and father. There is no heir apparent to preside over the rituals to our Lords. Hereinafter, I will continue with our traditions. I will supplicate our Lords until that day when, at his desire, Lord Oloroon will anoint the Chosen One.

A Douen For Marie

Marie was frying bakes as sunlight faded and darkness rolled in like a million corbeaux heading for their roosts. She lit the kerosene lamp, stretched forth her arms to the baby-faced moon, and sang, "Is love, love alone that make King Edward give up his throne." She was filled with expectation, for she knew her man, Big Heads, would soon be home. He would eat his bakes, drink his cocoa, and before he could fall asleep in the rocking chair, she would undress, draw the curtain that separated the living room from the bedroom of the single room she rented, and lead him to her bed.

Bakes were piled high, and the cocoa-tea, and saltfish stew were steaming when Heads arrived. In the darkness he leaned his bicycle against the latrine wall and then blindly reached for the flambeau that he routinely placed on the floor each morning before he departed for work. He lit the flambeau, placed it on the patch of bare earth, then parked the bicycle in the latrine, and locked the door. Finished with his daily routine, he picked up the flambeau and, filled with the anxiety that had gripped him all day, walked up the grass trace to Marie's house. Holding the flaming torch above his head, he mounted the four rickety wood steps and grabbed the door handle before he snuffed the light out and pulled the door open. Marie was waiting for him; the scent of her cashmere bouquet soap saturated the room.

"And how is Miss Sweetness?" Heads greeted her. Marie stepped forward and hugged him like a mother would a lost child. He tossed his hat on the table, scratched his big scraggy head, and before she could kiss him to set the evening's mood, he sank heavily into the rocking chair, placed his elbows on his knees and his head in his hands. Like most stevedores, Heads was perpetually tired. He toted sacks of sugar by day, drank rum in the evening, and craftily juggled a relationship with three village women. He remembered a time when his lifelong dream was to become a bus driver. That was when he was married and lived in London. That all ended with his return to Trinidad to attend his grandfather's funeral. Because of his grandfather's long years of service on the Port-of-Spain wharf, Heads had the opportunity, as next of kin, to apply for the stevedore job.

Marie knelt beside the rocker and began to untie Head's shoes. "I have your bath water ready, you know," she cooed, gazing intently into his face as she dragged the heavy boots from his feet. "You could eat first or bathe first, whichever one you want to," she said. It suddenly struck her how much Heads resembled the one child she had for him. How she wished she could have another child for Heads.

"It happen' again, Marie!" Heads groaned, oblivious to her flirtation to eat or bathe. Startled, Marie jumped to her feet. "What happen, doodoo?"

"I can't believe what this world coming to." Heads shook his head in disbelief.

"What happen, doodoo? They calling strike on the wharf again?" Marie stepped behind the rocker and placed her braided head against his, her arms around his neck.

Visibly alarmed, she remembered the last stevedore strike when Heads fell two months behind on her rent.

"Girl, you home all day and you ain't hear what happen?"

"Here in Carenage?"

"Yes, it happen again. Right here in Carenage. They can't find Elfred!"

"Oh my God!" Marie gasped, backing away from Heads, her hand to her mouth, her eyes wide with fear. "Don't say that Douen gone with another child, doodoo!"

In the lamplight, Big Heads' jaw dropped. "Marie! You have to stop believing in them supernatural stupidness. You think people in London believe in Jumbie, Soucouyant, and all that foolishness? If the child you had for me was alive today, it would be as old as Elfred—seven years. You say is Douen take the child and kill it. I say is stupidness. Something else to blame, and I can't stop thinking about poor Elfred."

Marie dragged the cane chair to the table and sat down. She wiped her eyes. For years she had listened to Big Heads' complaints about his only child. Perhaps Heads was extra vex about the loss of his child since Heads was the only survivor from a brood of nine. She always thought Heads had survived by the sheer power of his physique. At six feet eight, he was the strongest and darkest stevedore on the wharf. When he told her his father's mother was white, she laughed and said, "Heads, your mother make a mistake, boy." That response caused Heads to isolate her for a month. He would eat, drink, and sleep, but not one word did he utter to her. Yet she often wondered how come Heads was the color of charcoal when his grandmother was white. This was a puzzle that perplexed Marie; at the thought of it she would shake her head, wring her hands and suck her teeth.

"Heads," she said with resignation, "one hundred times I tell you is Douen take your child. The night before the child die, I dream I see the child in Kiddies Carnival playing 'Mas' with some strange children. At first I didn't care, because Carnival have plenty strange children. But when I watch the children closely, I see some funny ones with straw hats on their heads and their feet turned backwards. I get frighten and rush in the band to take out my child. But before I could grab him, the children take off, a straw hat boy holding and dragging my child behind him. My child was snatched from me. Oh, God, this is the truth. Heads, you don't believe in bad, but we have bad right here in Trinidad, in Carenage. Next morning when I wake up, I find the child dead. I tell you so time-after-time-after-time, and yet you still doubting me."

Seemingly filled with pain, Marie watched Heads' expression through the slits of her fingers. How could she tell him that within days of the child's birth she had withdrawn her breasts and began feeding the child lime-bud tea? She loved her child, but the big head baby was born with teeth. He had powerful jaws and chewed on her nipples. Breast feeding the child was an ordeal. When she talked to Heads about her predicament, he became furious. "All women feed their baby from the breast. Give the child breast too!" he insisted. She had tried, but when she could no longer take the excruciating pain, she withdrew her breasts. After one month of lime-bud tea the child died. Filled with grief and guilt, she hid in her room for months.

Marie got up and went to her bed. Because Heads did not follow, she had to lie upon her starched and pressed white sheet alone. The preparations she had so carefully made to entrap Heads into love making, and with God's help, to get another child, were extinguished by Heads' pain and complaints. Minutes later she could hear him snoring in the rocking chair.

⋙⋘

The following morning Marie left home to join the search for the missing Elfred. A dozen villagers had already assembled at the rum shop. Among them were Mother Nella; Papa Wenge; the rum shop owner, Boisman; Monrepos, and others. After a flurry of greetings and a few fast and furious rums, the villagers set out to find the abducted Elfred. The search party crossed the Chaguramas Road and began a steep climb that seemingly would take them into the clouds. Bacanoit and gru gru bouef trees towered overhead, while on the ground thick and almost impenetrable lastro covered the ground. Yet they climbed higher and higher, their shouts of "Elfred! Elfred!" filling the air as they beat the lastro and combed the ravines. The yellow sweet oil and the rainbow-colored snowball butterflies escaped the beaten bush to flutter helplessly around the Elfred searchers. Chameleons peered down from the mango trees and snakes, the tigre and bushmaster bolted to escape the crashing feet and bush-beating search party. Halfway up the mountain they advanced on a troop of howler monkeys who threatened to beat them with branches before the monkeys disappeared in the forest of trees. The village search was in vain. Six hours later, their skin burning from stinging-nettle and mosquito bites, they abandoned the search and headed down the mountain to regroup at the rum shop.

"Marie, girl, you is a hero," Monrepos said, to her surprise. "I spend two hours searching and had to run from heat and that climb. You spend a whole half day, and you still looking fresh. Girl, you is a hero."

"Hero or not, this is not time to make joke, Monrepos," Marie said. "Is a child the Douen take, and we must do everything to rescue him. On top of that we should do something about these Douen that spiriting away we children."

"I think we should get a priest," Sharkman said.

"Forget the priest," Monrepos said. "Which priest coming down here?"

"If you pay a priest, he will go anywhere," Sharkman said.

"We could get a priest on Saint Peter's day. Every priest and pastor does come to Carenage on St. Peter's day," Marie said. The conversation petered out and Marie ordered a beer. She sat on a sweet-drinks box and taxed her brains as to how best they could find the missing Elfred.

The sun had disappeared behind the mountain and was set to plunge into Chaguramas Bay when Marie entered her home and began to prepare dinner. She cleaned and seasoned the cavalli, and while it marinated in the lime juice and sliced tomatoes she kneaded the flour for the bakes. At dusk the village was set on fire with the news that Braverman had found Elfred and that the child was at the rum shop. Overjoyed, Marie set aside her bakes and cavalli and hustled up the village road.

Marie pushed her way to the center of the villagers who stood mesmerized while Braverman narrated his story. "I know we search the mountain," Braverman was saying, "but a voice keep telling me, 'Elfred up there, Elfred up there.' So I pick-up myself, cross Chaguramas Road, and climb the mountain again. It was about five o'clock when I reach a ridge a little higher than where we end the search when I hear a cry from the ravine below. I say to myself that sound like a child, Braverman. Boy, you better go and see. So I take my time, is a steep precipice you know, and I climb down to the ravine bed and follow the crying sound.

"When I reach near the sound, I see a cave, so I stop. You know is all kinda things you could find in a cave. Some have snake, some have bat, some even have spirit in them. Anyway, I pause at the entrance, wandering what to do. But I know I had to do something because I realize the sound coming from the cave was the cry of a child. So I tell myself, Braverman you have to check this out. So I gruff up my chest and walk in the cave as if I own it. Bam! The first thing I know is hundreds of bats pelting they selves from inside the cave to escape. So with bats lashing me from head to foot I take off from the cave. Hear nuh man, I really get frighten. But by the time I stop running I realize is only bat coming from the cave, and who fraid bat? Not me! So I double back and stop outside the cave mouth.

"Well, by that time every bat and he brother was gone. I walk like a man inside that cave, and you know what, who you think I see lying on the ground—Elfred! When I bring him out, I never see that, the boy whole body crisscross with scratches. He face was a spider web pattern. It look as if something with long fingernails scratch Elfred from head to foot."

Marie stood spellbound, fascinated by the story. She had no doubts about the scratch marks; it had to be the work of one of the hundreds of Douen, the spirits of children who died before they were christened, roaming the mountains of Trinidad's Northern Range. Elfred had lost his voice, but Marie believed that when he recovered he would tell of his ordeal and certainly prove her right. However, little did Marie know that Elfred would never tell his story. From that day onwards Elfred never spoke again.

Marie rushed home and finished her preparations for Heads' evening meal. Thick slices of cavalli and warm bakes covered the flowered and white enamel plates; while perched between the two plates was Heads' white enamel cup filled to the brim with hot, steaming cocoa.

A short time later, Marie heard the familiar creak of her doorsteps. Ah, she thought, Heads was finally home. As was her habit, she went to the door, bent and put an eye to the keyhole, and waited for him to appear and pull the door open. Minutes passed, but there was no pull on the door. Then, instead of the doorstep creak, she heard the hinge on the latrine door squeal. Puzzled, she wondered, did Heads climb the steps and return to the latrine? She cupped her hands to her ears and listened intently, hoping to get an answer. From the darkness outside a moan filled her ear. Marie jerked upright. She stepped from the door and froze. She was certain somebody was at the door, on her doorstep. Another whimper floated to her ears, and with it came a scratching on the door. Alarmed, Marie drew a sharp breath.

Why Big Heads would scratch and not pull the door, she wondered? But then the next sound puzzled her even more—the cry of a baby. Hesitant, but filled with curiosity, Marie pushed the door open and looked into the darkness. A figure was sitting on the doorstep. Impulsively Marie called out, "Big Heads, is that you?" A child responded with a whimper. "Heads is that…." The child whimpered louder. Marie froze. She realized the figure on her door step was not Heads but a child.

"Who is you!" Marie said sharply, "Who is you!"

"Is me," the child moaned.

"Is me who?" Marie said as she rushed inside to fetch her lamp. Yes, she was right, she thought. The big head of the stranger had fooled her into thinking it was Heads who was sitting on her doorstep. But who was this child, she wondered. She returned with the lamp and held it up.

"Look," she said sternly, "who is you? Turn around and watch me!" The child refused.

"I say boy or girl or whoever you is, I will beat you! I say turn around now. Face me!"

The child turned. Marie screamed and dropped the lamp on the door step.

Big Heads, his lighted flambeau on the ground, had finished parking his bicycle in the latrine and was locking the door when he heard Marie scream. He looked up to see the kerosene lamp explode on the door step. Filled with Alarm, he shouted, "Marie!" then grabbed the flambeau and hurried towards the house. He was halfway up the trace, shouting "Mari! Marie!" when a figure, wailing like a baby, sped towards him. Surprised but determined to catch the oncoming culprit who must have frightened Marie, Big Heads straddled the track and held his flambeau high. The figure neared and was about to collide with Big Heads when he cried, "Ai! Stop!" In the flambeau light instead of grabbing the figure, Heads nearly fainted when he recognized the culprit, his child, Marie's baby dead these past seven years, dash between his outspread legs.

"Douen!" Big Heads bawled and pelted the flambeau at the fleeing child. Out the yard and up the road the child went, screaming and wailing in the darkness, a pack of yelping village dogs in hot pursuit. Breathless, trembling and moaning with emotional pain, Heads stood on the dirt track struggling to regain his sanity. He could think only of the terrified child, his child, pursued by dogs, curly haired and white like his Irish grandmother.

Zeitgeist 2009

"Everybody blaming the government for crime, but nobody looking at what they as individuals doing about crime. Crime is not only the government problem, crime is everybody problem." Peter Nemiah Muckup chaired the meeting. Dressed in big red Art Smart tailored shirt, he spoke loudly, as if to an audience in Woodford Square, and not to the four people, one woman and three men, who sat indignant, eager to hear Nemiah's plan for combating crime in Gorilla Crescent, a small village on the outskirts of Port-of-Spain. Jacob Taka, Nemiah's tenant and father of nine, was moved to speak up.

"I addressing crime in my own way, Mr. Chairman. But I ain't getting help from the government. In fact, instead of the government helping me up they helping me down. I cut Freddie ass for stealing four Julie mango from Miss St. Rose, and you know what, is I the police come looking for. Child abuse they say, for straightening out a upcoming thief."

"But Mr. Taka, you should understand the government's position on child abuse. The government recognizes that a beaten child models his behavior on his beating parents, and so, generation after generation, instead of curbing their children's behavior, by beating the children the parents perpetuate the violence that we, even at this moment, are trying to cure."

"Well said, Mr. Hardeed!" Chairman Nemiah tapped the table in agreement. His wife Alice, the lone woman in the audience, clapped and murmured "Amen!" a half-dozen times. Mr. Taka appeared bewildered. Like Mr. Forthright, Alice Muckup, and Mr. Hardeed, Mr. Taka sat in the first row of ten metal folding chairs with the other forty-five empty seats at his rear.

"All I saying is that that is my little way of tackling crime; my contribution to solving this massive crime situation in Trinidad. 'Bend the tree while it young.' That is what the old people say. It was true yesterday and it is true today," Mr. Taka said.

"I feel a different way," Mr. Fortright said. He lived in the four-bedroom house at the village entrance, the one with the high, white stucco wall crowned with blazing warratal rocks. He was a QRC boy, a skilled debater, and a geologist. To villagers that explained the unusual wall. "We should tackle crime from the bottom up and not from the top down as we are now doing."

"Meaning what Mr. Forthright?" Chairman Nemiah said. "I mean, that is what we are doing here. The government fighting at the top, and we fighting at the bottom, is that what you mean?"

"Yes and no. The government fighting, but they should fight different. Take, for example, the condition of mothers, especially young mothers, or the old people situation. I know resources are available for greater help. They should be treated much better."

Mr. Hardeed stopped picking his teeth, a look of consternation upon his face. He had heard this defense before, what he described as liberal refuse fit only for the Labasse.

"You mean the government should pamper people who instead of taking responsibility totally ignore it and then blame the government," Mr. Hardeed said. He lived at Santa Rosa Heights and owned a haberdasher business on Charlotte Street. Scouting the constituency for occasions to meet and address groups of people, he had stumbled on Nemiah's "Crime Watch" meeting and was the first to arrive.

"You talking about young mothers, or you talking about old people?"

"Both, Mr. Forthright," Mr. Hardeed snapped. He was a no-nonsense Tobagonian and a mirror image of the Diego Martin West Parliamentary representative whom he sought to replace. "Young girls don't have to get pregnant!" He swiveled in his seat and addressed Mr. Forthright directly. "They choose to get pregnant. For them responsibility is a four-letter word. Do it and let somebody else take the responsibility, and that somebody else is the same government that the opposition beating up on like a Good Friday Bobolee and saying the government could do more."

Mr. Hardeed turned and addressed Chairman Nemiah, "The government building thousands of houses, you know, and they saying the government should build more."

"And what about old people?" Mr. Forthright said, disgust for Mr. Hardeed showing on his face.

"Well, old people is a horse of a different color." Mr. Hardeed crossed his legs, straightened his tie, and addressed Chairman Nemiah. "You know, Mr. Chairman, you have people in this country that never lay a hand on a shovel," he said with incredulity. "Never lay a hand on a shovel. Some play card, some sleep late, some smoke weed, all some do is drink rum—and thanks to this government some drinking whisky, drinking Double Dog like water today! They too proud to work." Mr. Hardeed paused. He eyeballed the participants for signs of agreement. And, except for Mr. Forthright, nodding heads told him he had it. He smirked and continued his diatribe against the poor. "When you say 'Work!' is like you cuss they mother, boy. Imagine that. Work for them is not pride in standing on one's feet; work is a four-letter word, something you do to them instead of something you do for them. And so after thirty, forty, fifty years they retire with nothing to show for it except nine children, nineteen grandchildren, and no pension. That is their fault, man."

On Mr. Taka's face bewilderment turned to outrage, the condition that once made him chop-off the right hand of a man. "Mr. Chairman," he said, "that sound like Mr. Hardeed talking to me and the nine children I make—I work! I pay rent! I feed my wife and children!"

Mr. Hardeed had blundered. He was at the meeting to praise the Prime Minister and defend the government with the hope that the Prime Minister would hear of his efforts and choose him to be the candidate for the Diego Martin West constituency seat; one considered a sure win for whomever the Prime Minister chose. Mr. Hardeed was apologetic. He uncrossed his legs and addressed Mr. Taka directly.

"You try, Mr. Taka, you try. You work hard. You take care of your family. I don't mean people like you," Mr. Hardeed blundered on.

"But that is all he can do," Mr. Forthright moved to Mr. Taka's defense. He had experienced the plight of the poor in Gorilla Crescent, the overcrowded houses, the lack of recreation, the nightly gunfire, and the early morning pickups of dead young African men. He had attended both Mr. Taka's sons' funerals and as a result had become acquainted with Mr. Taka's seven surviving children.

"What you mean 'I try,' Mr. Taka said, anger welling up in his chest. He slammed his fist on the table. "I could get real vex you know…."

"Mr. Chairman, we need to hear your crime-fighting plan," Mrs. Alice Muckup cut in and brought her husband, Chairman Nemiah, back to his purpose. Curious villagers now peered through the windows of the Community Center. For them, meetings here were for the select few—a coterie of ruling party supporters.

"Thank you, my dear wife, for always advising her dear husband. Today, I expected about forty people, you know, seeing that crime is so severe and affecting everybody. But this small gathering, the five of us sitting and discussing here, is not the time and place to present what I consider a proper and workable plan. The Prime Minister is doing his part. He is hiring more police. He is building up the Army. We gone from one battalion to two. Maybe he will go to three and even four battalions. The Prime Minister buying fast patrol boats for the Coast Guard. He have a spy blimp, a real Crime Watch, in the sky. So he trying. He trying and we have to try too. But like I say, with only five people here, now is not the time to present my plan. So, I suggest that we meet again, with a promise that each one of us take on the task of bringing five people to the next meeting. And that is my plan for today," he laughed. "Do I hear an aye?"

"Aye," the quartet responded; and on that note Chairman Nemiah adjourned the meeting.

⤝⤞

That evening Mary, one of the Muckups two children, the other, Rougian a police officer, visited her parents and narrated the woe in her life. That morning her man, Santos, had pitched her out for the twenty-eleventh time, as Alice Muckup would later describe it. Along with her three small children, Mary had no place to go, except back to her parents' home.

"But what about Santos' mother house," Alice Muckup said. "Is a five-bedroom house she own in Macoya. How come she can't accommodate you? Them three children is she son own, you know."

"She say the children will break up she things, and they cuss too much," Mary said.

"What you mean they cuss too much," Nemiah said and stopped filling his hops bread with smoked herring. "Them is small children. One is five, one is six, and one is one. What kinda cuss they could cuss?"

"Daddy, they picking up cuss words from Santos. He don't care what he tell me. He cussing A word, B word, C word, F word. He cuss every word in the alphabet in front the children."

Mary sat hunched over a bowl of cereal, tears rolling from her downcast eyes, her cheeks heavy, her makeup on her washrag. She wiped her dripping nose and intermittently spooned corn flakes to her mouth. The six-year-old, five-year-old, and one-year-old ignored their bowls of Quaker Oats and stared at their eating, weeping mother.

"So why you come back here? The last time you come we had bacchanal." The family was seated in the kitchen—the adults at the table; the babies on the floor. "Santos threatened to kill your father. Now you expect we to go through that again?" Alice sugared Nemiah's tea and placed it alongside his hops bread on the flowered plastic tablecloth.

"Is we daughter," Nemiah said in resignation.

"But where we will put her? This house have one bedroom, a living room, and a kitchen. The adult children in this village adding they own room or building house in they parents' yard, but we don't have the space here. Rougian build up the downstairs and that is his home. So where will we put Mary and her three children?"

"Help me, Ma, I don't ever want to see Santos again," Mary sobbed. For the twenty-eleventh time, Alice remembered, Mary had said the same thing. In 2002 Mary was declared winner of the Gorilla Crescent beauty contest and was well on her way to contest the national Trinidad and Tobago beauty queen title when she became pregnant with her first child. In the beginning Alice had desperately tried to sabotage the romance between Mary and Santos. She went so far as to tell Mary the lie that Santos was a Buller Man. But even if she had told Mary that Santos was the man who had shot Richardson in his driveway, Mary would have continued the relationship.

"The last time you come you stayed six months. We don't have space here. We don't have a place to put you up. Go to Macoya."

Nemiah listened grim-faced. He thought the time had come to deal with Santos; to deal with Santos the way the

Trinidad and Tobago police dealt with gang leaders—they killed them. He should kill Santos himself, or get somebody to do it. The man make big money as a drug lord. But instead of minding his children, he keep throwing them out like Kentucky Fried chicken bones.

"I warn Mary you know, I warn her," Nemiah thought, "but she break stick in she ears. Now she in trouble again is me she looking to rescue her. Girl children don't listen. I listen to my mother. She tell me learn a trade. My father take me to a pipe fitter. I learned trade with him for five years, and that is why today I working with WASA. I feel to chop up Santos like King fish. But what to do? Mary is my daughter. She is we own—with my grandchildren. Yes, I could pay to kill Santos, but violence is not my head. I leave Santos in the hands of the Almighty. God will deal with him."

"Alice, we have to take them in. Is we children—all four of them. We have to forget the past; we have to look to the future; we have to take them in." He swallowed the last mouthful of Lipton, belched, and looked towards Alice with determination.

"But doodoo, we don't have space." Alice stood and whimpered to Nemiah. "These children will spread out in the living room like sausages dressed in pajamas. Somebody bound to mash them, and if is you in your size fourteen—they dead!" The remark broke the seriousness of the moment. The Muckups laughed, an infectious laugh that little Tina and Gerry caught. They too squealed with laughter. "You will mash them up, flatten out the sausages under the size fourteen." Alice laughed heartily, tears streaming down her face. "But I still say we don't have space."

"Yes, we have space," Nemiah said. He had found a solution to Mary's problem, and he laughed like the day he received his bonus. "Yes we have space, right here!"

"Here?" Alice spit out the words like a bullet from Rougian's Glock pistol.

"Yes, right here, in the backyard," Nemiah said.

"You mean the two-room house Taka renting?'

"Yes."

"Taka house? That one?"

"Yes, the same house, the green paint house, the house with the galvanize roof paint green, yellow, and red; the house with the wife, husband, and seven children. Taka have to go!"

"Nemiah, you crazy. You putting Taka out? We tenant who bringing in a little money to help you pay for the old car, have to go? Nemiah this is madness. This is massive madness."

Mr. Taka had always considered himself Nemiah's tenant for life. In fact, Mr. Taka had never even considered moving up to a bigger and better house, or even to build a house of his own, or even to apply for one of the thousands of houses Mr. Hardeed said the government was building. At any rate he could not build in Gorilla Crescent where, like Laventille, Morvant, and Dundonald Hill, every scrap of land was occupied. In Gorilla Crescent young adults were adding rooms to their parents' homes to house their families. He had counted forty-two people living in the house next door. Two of his five sons had been shot dead. But he had reorganized his life, relocated, and now, with his wife and seven children at Gorilla Crescent, for the first time he had felt secure. His ten-year jail sentence was behind him, and it did some good, it gave him rank, and secured him a permanent position in URP. He and his wife and children were happy, happy in their small, limited world at Gorilla Crescent. They had grown accustomed to this world. If scarcity of space was not a problem, so was scarcity of water and food. Mr. Taka would often mutter, "This place is cramped." He bought a bigger gold chain; but he never searched for a bigger house. He bought expensive sneakers; but he never searched for a piece of land. Gorilla Crescent was there, just like the Rose mango tree, and he loved it. He could smoke a joint and watch the Gru Gru Bouef palms float towards him and giggle. And he knew his children would grieve to death if they had to give up the cloud-high Rose mango standing between his house and Nemiah's. In fact, his thoughts focused on the day when his children would grow up and like a flock of Martiniquan Sickia depart his house and head for the tallest Pomerac tree; then he and his wife would have the house to themselves.

But Mr. Nemiah thought differently. "I say Taka must go," Mr. Nemiah said. "True, Taka does bring in a few dollars, but this is we flesh and blood. Taka have to go, and Taka have to go soon."

The moon was out, a crescent peeping through the black Bacanoit and plating Nemiah's house, like a tenor pan, with chrome. Howler monkeys once ruled here, but as the Port-of-Spain population increased, the howler population decreased until they were completely exterminated. How the village gained its name is filled with conjecture, but the most likely one is that howler monkeys were erroneously labeled gorillas, and so with a road that followed the crescent arc of a dry ravine from village entrance to mountain foothills, Gorilla Crescent was born.

Days later when the moon hung like a curry calabash above the highest peaks, another meeting was called to order. Two dozen people were present. Chairman Nemiah was elated. He thanked the originals for their homework. "Your dedication is the reason why we have so many people here this evening, and that in spite of rain showers in the middle of this supposedly dry season."

But there was one person of the original five who was missing—Mr. Taka. Mr. Nemiah felt unhappy about that, but he had no doubts as to why Mr. Taka was absent: he had given Mr. Taka notice to move. His daughter and children needed a place to live, he had explained to Mr. Taka, and having no alternative, he had to house them in Mr. Taka's place.

"The plan! The plan!" A voice shouted through a window that woke Chairman Nemiah from his momentary lapse into reverie. An unruly group had gathered outside the Center, a development that Chairman Nemiah had not anticipated. Soon, the outsiders were on the inside, filling up the Center, calling for more chairs, scuffling and bantering with one another. They never settled down, yet demanded Chairman Nemiah present his plan. "The plan! The plan!" they shouted, putting a fear in Nemiah that he had too often felt as a child. Angry, shouting men always terrified him and made him feel to run like a monkey with a mongrel at its tail.

"What is the plan, Mr. Chairman?"

"But ghetto people unruly, eh," Alice Muckup addressed her husband, her remark lost in the commotion. She regretted her past elections canvassing of the squatters, the late comers who had arrived and built houses on the steep slopes which forty years earlier she and Nemiah had deemed impossible to build on when they first arrived in Gorilla Crescent. The squatters had come in five-year waves—purposeful voter increases for the party in power. In 1961 and for three decades they came from St Georges and Kingstown; in the late 1990s they arrived from Georgetown. And because they were considered mere ballots—schools, hospitals, houses, roads were never built to accommodate them. At this meeting, however, the squatters were not the originals but the descendants. Unlike Mr. Nemiah who was a bona fide government tenant, these squatters—seduced and abandoned—existed like the howlers they had replaced: they were a law unto themselves. Here the police never set foot unless to secure a body at daylight, often after it had been desecrated by marauding dogs.

"The plan!" the newcomers bellowed, "What is the plan, Mr. Chairman?"

"The plan," a standing Chairman Nemiah shouted, "is a massive march against crime! That is the plan. We will march from Gorilla Crescent to Port-of-Spain and back. Every organization is doing it. Every village is doing it. And we will do it too!"

"The Chairman is a mad man. Aye, we talking about hanging bandits! Shooting gunmen! Decapitating dope pushers! And the chairman talking about a march on crime! Come on, man. You better than Tommy. You joking." The Rasta Man was adamant. On his head was a woven red, yellow, and green hat; but blood and slaughter was on his brain. The criminals like the howlers were pests to be exterminated. "Kill the drug lords! Kill the gang leaders! Kill the gunmen!" he shouted to deafening applause. Excitement filled the air. People danced, shook their fists in defiance, and cried, "Death to the drug dealers."

And although he shouted himself hoarse, it was evident that Chairman Nemiah had lost control. "No violence!" he shouted. "Please, no violence! Not me, I will have no part of violence." His world was that of the obedient, the law-abiding, even if the laws against marijuana and cocaine were now irrelevant, an ass.

Mr. Forthright had seen it coming. He sat in silence, staring at the throng and wishing for calm. The time had come, he thought, the people were ready to act, to take on the gang leaders, the gunmen, the dope pushers—the winners in the war on crime. These screaming men and women were in fact the law-abiding of the burgeoning ghettoes— the carpenters, masons, steel benders, cooks and maids who kept the country humming. These were the people who took to the road at fore-day morning to build the "skyscrapers," the idiots' projects, calculated to boost self-esteem and substitute dither for development. These were the people whose steel bands had been hijacked by "sponsors." And like the middle class, Mr. Forthright too once believed that the ghettoes were created by the people who lived there, and that they were all incorrigible troublemakers and lawbreakers, the source of the country's breakdown. "Could anything good come out of Gorilla Crescent?" the *Newsnight* newspaper had asked rhetorically.

Mr. Forthright now thought differently. His sojourn at his grandfather's house at the village entrance had changed his views: just as Federation Park was the home of big actors, so too the ghetto was the home of small actors. The big actors wore jackets and ties; the small actors were costumed as Rasta, Rapper, and Ghetto Chick. The big actors had their "skyscrapers"; the small actors their dreadlocks, gold chains, and plastic fingernails. The ghetto was a response to rejection; the gaters, terrified behind high concrete walls and electric fences, an appeal for imperial inclusion. These people, Mr. Forthright thought, were today's Shouter Baptist struggling against British oppression in post-independence Trinidad and Tobago. Beneath the fierce Rasta and Rapper and foul-mouthed Chick was a Trini nationalist: a Trini by boat but a Trini to the bone. These screaming men were ready and willing to seize control and defend their wives, children, and communities. Increasing the armed battalions was nothing more than a shrewd gater hedge against the coming rebellion; for what other reason could explain the increase in military power? Mr. Forthright looked up, startled. Chairman Nemiah was calling on him.

"Mr. Forthright! Mr Forthright! Aye, sir, you want to address the people? This is too much unruliness for me. Ladies and gentlemen, Mr. Forthright will address you." Like a basketball, he tossed the meeting to Mr. Forthright. Mr. Nemiah had had enough of the ghettoists, as Alice had labeled them. He wished they would leave Trinidad. Whether first, second, third, or fourth generation, they should just pack up and leave Trinidad. Someday, he hoped, when votes and nothing else but votes concerned the government of the day, a leader would have the courage to pick them up and ship them out. These were the people who made him feel damn blasted ashamed to give his address as Gorilla Crescent. He and his wife were good people who had to suffer because of these ruffians.

Mr. Forthright, though filled with trepidation, took a defiant stance. He clapped his hands, thumped the table with a Solo bottle, and entreated the mob to calm down.

"People! People! People! Ladies and gentlemen, please…," he shouted. "Give me your ears, your attention for a moment, please." The mob was in a raucous mood. Rowdy election campaigns were the people's only political experience. When it came to parliamentary procedure, they were illiterate—every man was a chairman, every woman a chairwoman. Mr. Forthright steeled himself. He would have his say, and Eric Williams be damned.

"What this country calls for is a government knowledgeable enough to attack the problem of crime with the creation of programs that emphasize human development!" Mr. Forthright shouted above the din. "Human development! That's right. Human development! That's what I say. What is missing in this country, in Trinidad and Tobago, is a recognition that we need to develop, to humanize, to empower our most precious resource—the people. We are all humans, but what is missing in this our beloved country is humanized behavior. When a brother shoots a brother at point blank range and laughs, that is self-hate. That is dehumanized behavior! And to demolish this behavior we must trust the people. We must love the people. We must care for the young, the aged, the poor! We must integrate the ghettoes into the national community. And we must empower the people; devolve power to the people! That's right! Devolve power to the people and let them run their communities!"

"No big words," the red, yellow, and green woolen-hat Rasta shouted. "If is revolution, say REVOLUTION! Man. I am for that!"

"We don't need more development. We have enough development in the country," a gray-haired URP veteran said. "Watch the Hyatt and the Crown Plaza on the Port-of-Spain wharf. What we need is…." The mob was right on cue.

"Action!" they shouted.

"What we need today is…."

"Action!" the mob shouted.

"What we need tomorrow is…."

"Action!" the mob howled.

Mr. Hardeed at first smiled, then unable to contain himself, he guffawed. Chairman Nemiah was aghast. He motioned Mr. Forthright to sit, and when Mr. Forthright stood his ground, Chairman Nemiah stabbed his finger in the direction of Mr. Forthright's chair and insisted that he sit down. Once a champion QRC debater, Mr. Forthright had no choice but to take his seat. He choked on his tears. Emotion had beaten reason.

Soon the mob was singing the Trinidad and Tobago national anthem and waving sweat-scented washrags. When Chairman Nemiah ignored protocol and called for silence, it was Mr. Forthright, despite his defeat, who motioned him to stand and be silent. Mr. Hardeed, hands clasped behind his back, his belly collapsing onto his belt, stood at attention. He eyed Mr. Forthright, savoring the sweet taste of victory. The anthem ended, the crowd began to chant PNM! PNM! PNM! And without consent from the chairman, Mr. Hardeed spread his arms and took control of the chair. Mr. Nemiah could not believe it. In all the years he had chaired his PNM party group meetings, he had never encountered a more energized group than this. It seemed the beginning of what Mr. Forthright called the revolution, and it was terrifying. His chairmanship snatched from him, Mr. Nemiah felt he had no choice but to take an exit. He and Alice plunged into the mob and struggled towards the door.

If it was a moment Mr. Nemiah dreaded; it was the moment Mr. Hardeed had waited for. He shouted, "PNM or die!" The mob loved it; they responded, "PNM to the bone!" Opportunity had fallen to Mr. Hardeed's hands like a Rose mango with smiling cheeks. He was there to secure his candidacy, for votes, and these were votes for the picking. He gestured for order. The same order Chairman Nemiah had shouted for and could never get, Mr. Hardeed got in an instant. It could have been his briefcase, which he twirled aloft, or his dark shades, or his PNM balisier tie. The unruly crowd, now numbering some one hundred men, women, and children appeared sedated. In fact, they overly respected the Big Pappi—men in jackets and ties, and especially men in balisier ties.

"If the Peoples National Movement gained a majority in Parliament," Mr. Hardeed cried; "if a PNM majority is successful in this election, I tell you, you the good law-abiding people of Gorilla Crescent, the hangman would be banned from taking a holiday. I say no holiday, no vacation for the hangman!"

"No holiday, no vacation! No holiday, no vacation!" the mob picked up the chant and cheered Mr. Hardeed on.

"I say if the PNM win this election is licks like fire for the gunmen, licks like fire for the drug dealers! Licks like fire in they backside! They can run but they cannot hide." At this the crowd went into a frenzy. "P-N-M! P-N-M! P-N-M!" they chanted.

Alice was terrified. Were these the supporters of the party she had backed for forty years? The party of 'Intellectual chicken and wine'? She and Nemiah exited the Community Center as if they had been run out of Gorilla Crescent.

Change had come to Trinidad and Tobago—a furious wet season arrived and drowned out the dry. Rain showers flooded the Caroni plains. Sheets of water cascaded down the hills and valleys of the Northern Range. The Gorilla Crescent ravine overflowed its banks. Mr. Taka should have moved by May 31. But now it was early August, he still occupied the two-room house in the Muckups backyard. At first he had made a few passing enquiries about a room; then later he and his wife had made a concerted effort to find a place, even putting a flier in the "House of Judah" parlor at the village entrance. The last house-hunting attempt he made he had to cool his temper. He wanted to chop up the National Housing official, who, despite government advertisements of a house for all, for a third time rejected his application. Gorilla Crescent, like an overinflated tire ready to explode, had no land, no houses, no rooms to spare.

Mr. Nemiah had confronted Mr. Taka in June. He had confronted him in July. And now that it was late August, Mr. Nemiah prepared to confront him again. In the meanwhile Mary and her three children had seemingly settled into her parents' home forever. Mr. Nemiah now slept in the kitchen; Alice in her carved-out space on the living room floor. That was fine with the innocents; they along with their mother occupied the Muckups' bed. But just as Mr. Nemiah had confronted Mr. Taka, Santos had confronted Mr. Nemiah. Alice watched her husband seemingly turn grey overnight, and it was his fault, she thought. His troubles could have been avoided if he had not insisted on housing Mary. She had tried with Mary. When Mary on her first sitting of the Common Entrance exam scored low, Alice sent Mary to Mr. Forthright for tutoring. But either Mary's head was too hard or she was just more interested in boys than school; Mary again scored low on the exam. She graduated from Senior Sec reading like a grade three student. Asked what she wanted to do, she replied, "Anything except things having to do with maths." Mary once said that she feared maths even more than she feared snakes.

On September first the Prime Minister announced the November elections date. Alice supported Mr. Forthright, running as an independent candidate; while Mr. Nemiah supported Mr. Hardeed, the PNM candidate. Alice supported Mr. Forthright because he had helped Mary, but she also supported him because since Mr. Nemiah's first crime watch meeting in April, Mr. Forthright had opened a preschool for children ages two to six, at no cost to their parents. Despite free schooling for two of Mary's children, Mr. Nemiah, still a staunch PNM supporter, described Mr. Forthright's effort as "only trying to make the PNM look bad."

Nemiah listened to the Prime Minister's announcement on TV. He was satisfied. He decided on a visit to Mr. Taka. Thickets of Christmas and Black Sage bush sprouted among the razor grass in the backyard since he had stopped maintaining Mr. Taka's plot. He walked past the Rose mango and the goat tied to it and onto the narrow track that led up to the Takas. When he neared the house, Mr. Taka's mongrel attacked but soon went crashing through the Black Sage bush when Mr. Nemiah faked a stone throw at it. Mr. Nemiah reached the board house, climbed the three steps, and knocked on Mr. Taka's door. Someone had drawn on the green-painted cedar wood door a white shepherd with Afro hairstyle and red flowing robes holding a sheep and a staff with the caption, "Jah Lives." That drawing must have been the work of one of Mr. Taka's sons, for Mr. Taka had converted to Islam during his ten-year jail term. Mr. Nemiah ignored the drawing: his thoughts were on his tenant. He wondered why with seven children and two adults no sound was coming from inside the house. He had expected the noise made by cricket fans at the Oval, yet silence prevailed. He banged on the door again, with the sudden thought that maybe unknown to him Mr. Taka had moved out. Mr. Taka, however, was at home, and apparently prepared for Mr. Nemiah's visit. He had sent his wife and children to his sister's house for a stay until after he had finished with the Nemiah business. The door creaked open, and Mr. Taka, shirtless and in sliders, bid Mr. Nemiah an amiable, "Good morning, boss."

Mr. Nemiah was stunned. When he last confronted Mr. Taka, Mr. Taka had attacked like the Opposition Leader. He cussed Mr. Nemiah with vivid anatomical descriptions of his wife, daughter, mother, grandmother, and even his great-grandmother. Yet today Mr. Taka was sweeter than tooloom. What did this mean? Mr. Nemiah wondered.

"Mr. Taka, when you moving?" Mr. Nemiah, adding saccharin to outdo Mr. Taka's tooloom, said and smiled.

"I ain't moving." Mr. Taka was firm but spoke softly. He stood legs apart, one upraised arm leaning against the door frame, the other propped on his waist. "I tell you two-three-times already, I ain't moving. When you ready, just put me out. You is the boss," he laughed. "When you ready, pitch me out, but I waiting for your ass."

The menace in Mr. Taka's voice forced Mr. Nemiah to the offensive. He shivered; he wanted to shit. But he had to stand up to Mr. Taka. He had to be the lion in Judah. "Lord, God, what the France I have to deal with here! Who the hell is you? Mr. Taka, after the three months' grace I give you, you still ain't moving? You want me to throw your big black hungry ass out?"

Mr. Taka's response was calm. He was the lion, and he knew it, in fact everybody on the URP project knew it. "I say put me out when you ready. But I say, Boss Man, I ready for your ass, you know. So put me out when you ready." Mr. Taka took a backward step, reached down, then swiftly raised himself to his former position. But there was a change—a significant change. The hand once propped on Mr. Taka's waist now gripped a cutlass.

Mr. Nemiah jumped back. He fell hard, landing on his backside. But he was up in an instant, dusting his pants, breathing deeply, fearful, and prepared for flight. He had come in peace; now violence stared him in the face. Mr. Taka might have been grand charging, but his next words forced Mr. Nemiah to realize how dangerous a situation he was in.

"The next time you knock on my door your scruffy head will knock on my door steps," Mr. Taka said. "I say I ain't moving! If you don't understand that, then you will take what you get."

⚜

A week later, when the loudspeaker trucks were extolling the virtues of Mr. Hardeed across the Diego Martin West constituency, Rougian took a day off and stayed at home. A police officer, he was a member of an elite unit, Special Operations against Resistance and Terror (SOART) whose task was the detection and apprehension of "Big Fish," as the Minister of National Security had described his unit's mission. He was attentive to his parents and sister; he trusted them, even showing his father, Mr. Nemiah, the combination to the safe that held an assortment of weapons. But he stood aloof from his sister's perpetual problems and his father's fight with Mr. Taka. On the day he stayed home a visitor arrived—Santos with his entourage of bodyguards, gunmen ready and willing to shoot their grandmother at Santos command. Santos sat in his truck and called to Mary. She was not at home, yet Santos declared she was inside and that if she did not come out he would enter and drag her out. At the sight of Rougian, however, Santos changed his mind and sped away. But he was not done with Mary.

On the following day Santos was back. He met Mr. Nemiah at the front door and adopted a mood of conciliation. He only wanted to talk to Mary and pass on the fistful of dollars that he held for her and the children. Conciliation was not Santos' game; he was smart, tough, ruthless— the qualities that made him *the* drug lord from Morvant. To Mary's horror, her father let Santos in. No sooner was Santos inside when he grabbed Mary, who began to bawl. He threatened to kill her if she did not leave with him, and when she refused, Santos, his arm locked around Mary's neck, dragged her screaming towards the door. The once-laughing children now cried in terror, the eldest using his fist against Santos' leg. Mr. Nemiah, however, acted spontaneously. He seized Santos' dreadlocks and set him screaming like a pig.

On the outside, Gorilla Crescent was calm. PH taxi drivers, the local men who dared transport people to and from Gorilla Crescent, plied their illicit trade. Mr. Taka went past the Muckups' house. He heard screams, paused, shook his head and, smiling, trudged through the backyard bush towards his home.

Inside the Muckups' home, however, Santos struggled to free his dreadlocks. "Let me go old Nemiah Muckup! Let me go!" Santos cried. But Mr. Nemiah, now fearing for his own life should Santos break loose, hung on to the Rasta dreads, wishing they would leave Santos' head so he could escape his murderous son-in-law. But he knew he had to do more. Maybe he should bite Santos on the neck or kick him in the groin, yet all he could do was to hold on, terrified, screaming while Santos jerked him around the room like a puppet in calf-length FUBU denim pants and white

Nike sneakers. His head, seemingly on fire, Santos let go of Mary and began to struggle with Mr. Nemiah. Mary, freed, wasted no time. She hoisted the baby onto her shoulder and with toddlers screaming behind she escaped from the Muckups' sanctuary.

The taxi drivers continued to ply their trade, soliciting the people who had gathered to stare at the Muckups' bacchanal. Seated in the truck and staring ahead, the Santos gunmen kept a low profile.

Mr. Nemiah was no match for the young, powerful drug lord. Santos soon freed his hair, grabbed Mr. Nemiah by the head and slammed him against the front door. Then holding him by the foot, Santos dragged Mr. Nemiah through the shards of glass and wood to administer a series of ambidextrous Timberland kicks on his body. Done with Mr. Nemiah, Santos called out to the vanished Mary.

"I coming back for you tomorrow. You either come with me, or a bullet for you!" He boarded his truck, started the engine, and with smoking tires squealing, sped off along Gorilla Crescent Road.

⌐⌐

The following day, and for days too many to count, Mr. Taka would have a fit of laughter when he approached Mr. Nemiah's house. And for days Mr. Nemiah remained a recluse while Alice and Mary tended his wounds. He had black eyes, knots on his head and forehead, two broken ribs, and a sprained ankle. The humiliation was too much, and he averted his eyes from his wife and daughter. He knew he had to reclaim himself or forever be the object of disrespect from them, and the people of Gorilla Crescent.

⌐⌐

Election Day came and went as expected. Mr. Hardeed, leading several marches against crime as his campaign strategy, won with a total of nine thousand votes. The runner-up, a Mr. Lightfoot, the candidate from the other ethnic party, the UNC, received five thousand. Mr. Forthright, adopting the slogan "Humanizing for Transformation," gained a mere twenty votes, two of them from Alice and Mary.

꿈꾸

Seven weeks later, on Christmas Eve, Mr. Nemiah's wounds, except for his still aching ribs, were a thing of the past. Santos had yet to carry out his threat; Mr. Taka still occupied the backyard house; and Mary and her three children continued to occupy the Muckups' bedroom. Mr. Nemiah sat before the TV and drank straight Black Label rum, his daily self-abuse for not pursuing Santos and reclaiming his lost image of man of the house. He was alone, declining to attend the village steel band Christmas concert with Alice and Mary. The TV showed Santa harnessing reindeer at the North Pole; Nemiah wondered what would happen were he to confront Santos in Morvant and gun him down in the presence of friends. It was what he wanted, law or no law; he wanted a dead Santos, and he wanted to be his killer. His respect for the law was crumbling in the face of what he had come to realize, who he really was—Mr. Nemiah was a coward, a man used to shielding his cowardice by citing the law. He could see himself as a child running from every challenge to fight. His self-hate was palpable. He grabbed the Black Label bottle and exploded it against the TV screen. He had had it. He was tired of the good, law-abiding man masquerade. He would have none of it, even if it meant kill or be killed. And the man he wanted to kill this evening was Santos—but not before he confronted Mr. Taka for the very last time.

A steel band was playing Silent Night, and the voices of children put words to the music. Mr. Nemiah looked out the window and was surprised to see Mr. Taka's wife and children, walking single file as usual, go past the house and on to the road singing the Carol. The words "All is calm, all is bright" made him pause and reflect on his resolution. He ground his teeth and sighed. If Mr. Taka was not with his family, then he must be at home, alone, Mr. Nemiah thought. He got dressed, his intention clear; he would face down enemy number two—Mr. Taka. From the table drawer he selected a butcher knife and slipped it beneath his belt. He left the house and, wishing he had brought the kerosene lamp to light his way, stumbled into the darkness. At the Rose mango tree Mr. Taka's goat bleated a greeting. Mr. Nemiah spit out the goat stink, steered around the animal, and kept on his stumble towards Mr. Taka's house. "Oh, God, how I fraid Taka," he muttered. "I know he cut off a man hand and he promise to cut off my head. But I does get so frighten when I see him. Oh, Father, help me. Help me to stab him fast when he open the door." Moments later he was on Mr. Taka's doorstep and banging on the cedar wood door as if to mash up Jah's face.

"Mr. Taka!" he shouted. "Mr. Taka! Open up, is Nemiah, your landlord." Minutes passed as he listened for Mr. Taka's footsteps and the squeak of the door. When he heard a squeak, he withdrew the knife from his belt and held it ready to stab Mr. Taka in the heart. But Taka's door remained firmly shut.

"Mr. Taka! Mr. Taka!" he shouted and kicked again. This was the final confrontation. He had to do it. Wasn't Mr. Taka the one who heaped disrespect upon him? Wasn't Mr. Taka the one egging on his children to laugh in his face and giggle, "Morning, Mr. Coward." He banged on the door like a bailiff with an empty pocket. Again and again he banged and kicked. But there was no answer from Mr. Taka. Except for the grunting pigs in the backyard darkness, no one was at home. A jumbie bird hoot sent shivers along Mr. Nemiah's spine. He looked up. The stars, unusually tiny, as if in retreat, filled the sky. Maybe, Mr. Nemiah thought, he should just go out and destroy a pig—cut its throat and let it bleed to death. That would show Taka. Or better yet, destroy all the pigs along with Mr. Taka's precious goat. Under the cover of darkness no one would ever know that he was the destroyer. The dead goat would preoccupy Taka's children, make them unhappy, and stop them from giggling at him.

And then an idea he had never dreamed of grabbed him. If Mr. Taka wouldn't leave the house, then maybe the house would leave Mr. Taka. Mr. Nemiah, seized with the idea, stumbled through the darkness like a mad man. At the Rose mango tree the bleat of the goat was not a greeting but a cry of pain as Mr. Nemiah tripped and fell upon it.

Tripping and falling was a lifestyle the Takas carried like a cross. Streetlights were on Gorilla Crescent Road, but out in the backyard where Mr. Taka lived, darkness prevailed. Mr. Nemiah had cut off Mr. Taka's electricity, which was hooked up to the Muckups' home. When Mr. Taka complained, Alice Muckup simply said "No rent, no electricity."

Mr. Nemiah dragged himself from the goat and, after a few more spills, soon reached his home and entered. He grabbed a pack of matches and the can of kerosene he used for filling the lamps when electricity failed and returned to Mr. Taka's house. He was deliberate. He walked up the steps and bathed Jah, the red-robed shepherd, with kerosene. Finished, he struck a match and set the door on fire. He had committed arson, and as a respecter of the law, he knew what that meant. If he had to spend a lifetime in jail for one act, he thought, he would just as well spend a lifetime in jail for two.

Mr. Nemiah returned to his house, but instead of going upstairs to his own abode, he unlocked Rougian's door, entered his home and his safe, and pocketed Rougian's Glock pistol. Time was short. Villagers were already converging on his property to gaze at the back yard fire. He resolved to go to Morvant, find Santos, and shoot him. And out the back door he went.

The steel band was playing "Joy to the World," the notes spilling onto the air sometimes low sometimes loud as the air currents shifted in the valley. Mr. Nemiah boarded a route PH taxi at Gorilla Crescent and found himself in the company of three people. The passengers had heard about the board house fire which was now sending sparks into the black sky. The driver was convinced that the cause of the fire lay in Mr. Taka's lap.

"You know how often I hear people talking about Taka children playing with matches. Children like them would burn down a concrete house much less the dry board house in your backyard, Mr. Nemiah. You should of give Taka notice to move a long time ago. You should never rent to people with plenty children. If you did give Taka notice to move, your board house would be standing today."

"You mean it had a fire in the Crescent today?" the front seat passenger said.

"Not today, tonight! Any minute you will see the fire brigade coming to out it," the woman with the Christmas gifts in the back seat said. "Matches and children don't mix. You know how much people children and matches distress!" The driver's story went unchallenged. The passengers agreed with him.

Mr. Nemiah sat quietly, the Glock a heavy warratal stone in his pocket. If the police and the fire department believed it was children and matches that had burned down his board house, then he would escape jail. But that was a chance he would not take. The police might identify him as the arsonist, arrest him, and spoil his chances to kill Santos. He had burnt Taka's home down, and now he would kill Santos. That was his resolve, and he would not move an inch away from it. He was headed for Morvant, and Morvant was in his sight.

Across the Laventille hills the electric lights of big and small houses twinkled along with those of a handful of flashing Christmas trees. In Morvant a DJ was blasting 2009 Soca hits. Even with the Glock in his pocket and murder on his mind, Mr. Nemiah could not help tapping his foot to the sweet Soca sounds wafting down from hill to highway. He had gained his nerve; he would never look back, not even if Burroughs had come to arrest him. The taxi slowed to a stop. He climbed out, bid the travelers goodnight, and headed uphill into the DJ explosion. Despite the blast of the DJ, from every house he passed came the ever present boom of a stereo. The voices of men and the laughter of women and children energized him. Ten minutes later, his undershirt soaked with sweat, he stopped at D Hot Spot, a parlor protected by four-inch square BRC wire, and bought an RC. Cola in hand, he continued his uphill climb. Screaming children, at play, were crisscrossing the road when he reached his marker, the lamppost decorated from top to bottom with the balisier, the symbol of the PNM, pasted onto it, and ahead, Santos' big, rambling two-story house Mary had described. The house was a mansion, one fit for the families of wealth—the Sabgas, Gillettes, Warners. Mr. Nemiah paused, plucked the white rag from his hip pocket and wiped sweat from his face. He figured he was about five lamppost lengths from where he stood to the mansion, now lit up with flashing bands of green, yellow, and red bulbs hung on trees along with undulating chains of diamonds festooned along its eaves. Three hundred feet later, in the glare of a lamppost light, Mr. Nemiah had no trouble locating the six foot six, three hundred pound Santos and his entourage of bodyguards. Except for Santos' mansion, the surrounding houses, as if struck by a plague, were boarded up and abandoned. Mr. Nemiah's approach silenced the men. Always on the lookout, in daylight these gunmen could detect an enemy a quarter mile distant. In the darkness, at three hundred feet, Mr. Nemiah was recognized.

"Santos, look out. Mr. Nemiah Muckup!"

At the shout Mr. Nemiah pulled the Glock and fired. That shot was the signal that triggered a fireworks display. Blazing guns seemed to rise from every bush, tree, and abandoned house on the hill. Santos went down, the gunmen went down, Santos' girlfriend went down. The gunfire was merciless. Santos took fifty bullets.

It was an unlucky night for Santos, his girlfriend, and bodyguards; but even an unluckier night for Alice and Mary Muckup. For when the smoke cleared and members of the special police unit, SOART, entered the contested area to identify the dead, the first body Rougian identified was that of his father, a bullet hole in his forehead, the back of his head blown off. The following morning the *Newsnight* headline read: Police Fired upon Kills Five (Pedestrian shot dead in crossfire).

In Gorilla Crescent news of Mr. Nemiah's death spread like fire in a dry bamboo patch. At one thirty Mr. Forthright received the news from an inconsolable Mary, making sleep impossible for the rest of that night. At daybreak, when the brightest star waned in the east, he dressed, doused the Christmas tree lights on the veranda and headed for the Muckups' home. Except for a few stray dogs and the big-eye-grieve calling "Marylee" from the Rose mango tree, Gorilla Crescent was asleep. Alice Muckup was awake; however, her hair uncombed, her face shrunken from a sleepless night, her eyes red bird peppers protruding from a dark face, opened her heart when Mr. Forthright entered her home. She greeted him with the words that had cut a channel in her soul. "I tell Nemiah to leave Mr. Taka in his house," she sobbed. "I tell Nemiah leave Mr. Taka alone. Leave Mr. Taka in his house. But Nemiah wouldn't listen. 'Mary is we own,' he say and give Taka notice to leave. Now he dead, dead and done for…a husband any woman would pay to have—my husband. They kill my husband. Is only killing, killing, killing in Trinidad. Now they kill my husband. What will I do? God hear me!" she demanded. "I say God hear me! What will I do without Nemiah!" Alice Muckup was devastated. Mr. Forthright, in a moment when words failed the QRC debate winner, embraced Alice Muckup. With tears falling, he could only mumble, "This is God's way. This is God's way. This is God's way."

In April of the following year Alice and Mary moved from the house on Gorilla Crescent. Mr. Taka, his wife, and seven children relocated to a room in Laventille. Alice would miss the Community Center where for thirty years she had hosted PNM parliamentary representatives for Gorilla Crescent. But with her vote for Mr. Forthright, supposedly a secret ballot, she and Mary had become political village pariahs. In addition, Mary had become a recluse and taken to alcohol. People celebrated her drug man's death, but much as Mary tried to forget about Santos, his memory remained her constant companion. Mary loved her man. Maybe Santos' mother knew that too or maybe it was love for her grandchildren that pushed her to invite Mary along with her children and mother to live with her at Macoya. Santos was an only son. When the police released his body, he was taken to Macoya where his mother gave him a burial fit for a prince. Alice Muckup, despite what seemed an unrecoverable catastrophe, showed her mettle. She applied for a URP job and was given a permanent position, a payment most people believed for her long and faithful service to the PNM. In Gorilla Crescent Mr. Nemiah's death seemed a catalyst for murder. On three consecutive nights following his death three young African men were gunned down.

Edmund Narine was born in Port-of-Spain, Trinidad. In 1970 he immigrated to the United States. He is a graduate of Boston University's Creative Writing Program. His first collection of short stories, *Mudrites and Mildew*, was published in 1994.

Made in the USA
Charleston, SC
24 April 2011